Pips
Arrington

1

Hypnocrite

Of Patients and Puppets- First Do No Harm

by Piper Arrington

International Standard Book Number

978-0-9970240-8-1

EPILOGUE ONE

EPILOGUE TWO

EPILOGUE THREE

GENESIS

Vinnie the Weasel

It is a grave misconception that all mob employees drop the F-bomb every other sentence. Vinnie is an even greater paradigm because he does not curse at all. Not even a little. No shit. No hell. No dammit.

He is a reliable, effective muscle man with 17 kills and an unknown number of maimings yet he never quite speaks the language. As Vinnie himself states:

  "If'n I slashes youse throat, that is a bidness transaction, a necessary thing. And I am good at my bidness, but I will not kiss my mother with a filthy mouth."

 And he won't. He is way too Catholic for that. Cradle Catholics fear and revere three things: the Virgin Mary, their own mothers and God the Father-in that order. Vinnie would never lay lips that have let the F-bomb blow out on his devout matriarch. That would be a sacrilege.

Vinnie has never experienced a conscience. He doesn't know what it is. A born and bred New Yorker, he came up on the east side of Harlem, and he had a working knowledge of the mob before he learned to read.

 The life is not a separate entity, it is his very breath.

 As a young boy, he ran errands for men who ran the rackets for the big men in suits and Vinnie delivered messages.

He still does the same job but the messages aren't written in graphite any longer. These he delivers with his fists, small iron casings or perhaps something even more inventive. Vinnie enjoys his work and so he is surprised when the anxiety attacks begin to appear.

At first, he ignored them, but last month, he was a given a hit on Tommy the Mick O'Toole. Like any good fella, he retrieved the package and set about his bidness. Tommy conceded to his fate after a brief plea for his life. Begging and bleeding, he tried to appeal to Vinnie's humanity. Problem is, Vinnie does not have much and still he hesitated, his heart palpitating 185 beats a minute with sweat pouring down his back. Tommy the Mick almost escaped his imprisonment.

I gots to get some help. Is there even a doctor for this?

On the Street

Inconceivable. Absolutely, irrefutably inconceivable. In this place in history, I cannot make a move without being tracked by my Iphone (traitor!) and yet I can still access a public street with a blonde wig, floppy hat and monstrous sunglasses. Take that, Big Brother, take that! It is so Charles Manson because I look like one of his sheep. Like cattle moving in unison too dumb to realize the power and release of free will. Says the woman hiding in a wig. Whatever it takes to thwart paparazzi….

The headlines would be endless if I was caught entering this place. I can imagine it now:

Calliope Cash Sees Hypnotist-Details Inside!

Exclusive: Calliope C. Has Gone Nuts!

With the byline: Her psychiatrist says so!

Hell, what am I supposed to do? I so get that bell jar reference now, Sylvia. I was not a big fan of you in high school when you were required reading, but now, here, in this spot light-I so get it. I am but a display, no deeper than anyone's eye can go. And there is absolutely no privacy here. It is stifling.

It is funny how I never pictured myself as a camera whore. My finite lobe could only conceive of the level of conceit it would take to pursue such a career as this. I guess I can rest in the knowledge that it indeed pursued me.

Calliope Cash, a rising New York model, popular enough to grace <u>Vogue</u> and have photographers trailing her but not quite to supermodel status, continues down the sidewalk in disguise. As if a wayward Chinook had blown in, this March day has turned into a bit of a scorcher. Due to the unexpected heat wave, the wig is quite uncomfortable and she pulls at it a little too often to maintain the anonymity she is seeking.

As a result, a member of the press who is wise to the tricks of celebrity, snaps a few quick shots of her as she passes by a local Starbucks. He is already constructing the headline in his mind as the shutter sings its symphony of images.

NO CAFFEINE FOR CALLIOPE.

He loves playing with alliterations.

Inconceivable, he thinks. *That at this moment in time, she thinks she can hide behind a blonde wig and a floppy hat.*

The photographer continues down the busy sidewalk scanning for his next victim, um, subject matter. His level pace quickens to a skip and then a run when he spots Tom Hanks ducking into the M&M store. Calliope continues on solo, unaware she was just photographed into seventeen images. She will discover it the same time everyone else does-when the magazine hits the stands.

Peyton Jane

Peyton Jane, if you ask anyone, is a great wife. PJ, her familiar name, is still a looker. No one person ever successfully guesses her true age of 48 nor that she has two grown children in their twenties. No lines have yet dared to cut deeply across her face. Peyton knows it is only the result of hair dye and good wrinkle cream. Each morning she traces the puppet lines on her mouth, sighs, and starts on the first of five bottles of water she will consume that day. The water may also contribute to her youthful appearance.

She takes meticulous care of her husband whom she adores and even better care of the beautiful home in New Jersey he has provided for her. It sits cock-eyed on a quaint cul-de-sac where similar brick mansions are spattered. She has help to keep the three floors and the mother-in-law residence immaculate. The worker comes just two mornings a week but she does windows and tubs and toilets. PJ never dirties her hands on those areas. She does not take the things Brad provides for her for granted. PJ knows how blessed her existence is.

 The children are grown and gone and so PJ takes this pre-grandchildren opportunity to dote on her man. She supports his every cause and meets each need regardless of which room in the house it entails. Their marriage, their love is the example most younger couples around them admire. No one would ever suspect what PJ is contemplating. That does not really describe it. It is consuming her. And she hates herself for being so weak.

PJ has not actually acted on anything yet, she just cannot stop thinking about it. She knows, because she reads women's magazines, that many housewives fantasize about celebrities and take those fantasies out on their husbands. She wishes that was all this was.

But she is intelligent enough to know it is way past that. She is consumed with the thought of another man. Not necessarily physically, although she has played that out mentally as well. He is brilliant.

Damn, Facebook. I would not be feeling this if I had not seen that post and imagined myself as the cause of it.

PJ is not one to hang on social media so it is simply bad luck that she even sees his post:

Unrequited love. No wonder so many writers have penned their best effort of unrequited love. I saw an old love of mine today. I imagine myself a braver version of me revealing how much I still carry. How I want to share it, hoping against hope that somehow it is known. I sense it so powerfully rising within me that I am the only one who truly knows how to cherish this love.

He does not name her. Thank God for that! She never even spoke to him in high school. But his simple entry stirs something old and deep that she did not know existed. This simple housewife is not swept away by an old acquaintance. She is swept away by his poetry. By the possibility that it COULD be her. That she might be more fulfilled. Yesterday her life was perfect. Today it is totally unsatisfactory.

How did this happen? How did I turn into a woman contemplating at the very least emotional adultery-may have already been guilty of that-when yesterday I was madly in love with my husband. He is a good man. An inherently good man. What has changed? How did one paragraph have such an effect?

But she knows that it has. PJ friends him and then spends the better part of her day googling this man who may or may not even know who she is. She copies the picture of him she finds most desirable. PJ has her own private Cyrano de Bergerac.

And then, dammit, he just had to post that poem.

The words that win her, tipping her into obsession and fantasy where no reasonable, well-adjusted woman would dwell.

That Poem

    I saw you this day

    You did not know because I could not move

    Not a lip nor a foot

    Your smile lit the night as you exited the film

    Alone.

I wanted to be there at your side

Touching your arm and escorting you

Sharing a look, that smile, your heart.

I should have been braver then

Back when I loved you so desperately,
without reason

Back when you did not know

And then I might be the man at your arm.

Cyrano posts some cryptic clues as to whom his love
is and PJ, having just been to see a movie and filling
all other empty blanks, allows herself to believe she is
the intended victim.

*Damn it and damn him! Am I too bold, too arrogant to
think he means me? What other woman can meet
that cryptic criteria: the movies, the marriage of 24
years, the two children, etc?*

And a voice, like conscience, whispers……

Thou shalt not lie with thy neighbor's wife. Leviticus
18:20

Yeah, yeah, I know!

Physically, this man is no match for her husband but
her connection to him is so much deeper than the

physical. Peyton Jane is in love with his mind and with his words and with that soulful look in his grey eyes. Her new infatuation disgusts her. It isn't who she is, who she has been or even who she wants to be. PJ picks up an issue of Time searching for some truth, some insight into her frailty and lack of willpower.

It is in the table of contents, an article about local New York physicians and their flourishing practices. She skims past the OBGYN and begins reading about Dr. Steven F. Fisher, MD.

Dr. Fisher

Steven is an adequate practitioner. At least, he used to be. He never expected to be so susceptible to corruption. But success is a poisonous dart and the venom travels in a slow seep. No child ever imagines they need toys like yachts and Ferraris, but once you can afford them, you don't understand life without them. It is almost like a beckoning, a call of the wild if you will.

Buy me, buy me, buy me…you know you want to.

And that feral nature responds but is never satiated by any one purchase. It wants more and then more sucking your soul like a thirsty vampire. Steven has moments of true clarity when he knows that he is more than his frivolity but the flesh fight always prevails. And now, his home has grown to the tune of 18,000 square feet and his garage can and does house six sports cars. One color for each day of the week except Sunday. On Sundays he still drives an old Jeep. He does not corrupt a Sunday. But not for any noble reason.

And a voice, like conscience, whispers:

Thou shalt honor the Sabbath and keep it holy.
Exodus 20:8

The voice to whom he refuses to listen.

Steven does not exhibit such restraint on any other day. Despite any other fault or flaw he may have, the good doctor ascribes to the idea a higher power.

Steven is all about power. He just prefers creating situations where he holds the most.

His first practice was modest and wrought with the debt of a fresh out of school physician with no clientele past his own sound and healthy family members. He studied hypnosis voraciously after watching a Vegas showman control three audience members. He was hooked. Not by the success of the performer's technique but rather the alarming sense of power one man held over another. His mind was swimming with the possibilities.

And so, three years later, he adds hypnotherapy to his practice promising to cure what ails ya' and the like. He has only minimal success at first because no one really believes in a quick fix. Nor do they buy mind control. And most people have some detail about their past they don't want to surrender to someone else.

 Steven does not concern himself with any one client's past while he is working with them. He is more interested in how he can orchestrate the present. He has become quite skilled at justifying his own behavior but his training is intensive on behavior disorders and so he already knows all the answers. And he believes his own PR.

He fondly recalls his initial client seeking treatment. He expected to see some withered old smoker wanting to rid himself of a cloudy demon. Instead, a frail thirty-something woman showed up with a desire to stand up for herself and say good–bye to the doormat she had been. In her marriage. With her parents. On her job at the DMV. She wanted to be empowered and Steven needed to feel powerful. Their sessions were intense and labored. But at the close of her therapy, Cheryl was a different woman, strong and able to speak for herself. She also almost immediately lost her job and soon after, her marriage. She threatened to sue Dr. Fisher for every cent but he, without her consent, re-hypnotized her and instructed her to completely forget all her therapy sessions with him. It was the perfect crime.

History Lesson

Three Years Earlier

Miss Honeycut, executive secretary to Dr. Steven Francis Fisher, crossed the elegant office area and strolled to the back of her oversized cherry desk.

 She has the gait of a girl who loves wearing a title with the word executive in it, one who is way too serious for her pay grade. This grand office complex where she works brings her great satisfaction as if she were responsible for the décor. Her left hand, well lotioned and velvety, pressed the left button on the intercom linking her desk to Dr. Fisher's. She has yet to call him anything more familiar.

"Dr. Fisher, I have confirmed your reservation for the Hilton in Las Vegas. I could not get the high roller suite but I managed to secure an excellent accommodation near the same floor."

"That will suffice, Miss Honeycut. Thank you for working on it," Dr. Fisher replied.

"Very well then, you will be departing from the airport at 7:00 am on Friday and returning on 5:45 pm on Tuesday. Do you need a rental or will you be leaving the Jeep on the terminal lot?"

"I will leave the Jeep. It will be more convenient for me."

"OK, then all is well. Have a wonderful time and spare me the details."

"You know what they say about the things that happen in Vegas," Fisher quipped.

"Umm hmm."

Even after two years of employment, Steven had never seen a smile on Honeycut's face. Honeycut was not attractive, not unattractive. Her appearance was always kempt but balancing the fine line of beauty. In the moment you discover a pretty thing about her, she speaks and you are struck by the whiney, nasal tone. It does not fit the package. She was proficient in everything and indispensable with the warmth of a slug. She never laughed at anything, not a joke or blunder. She was all business, all the time. Steven often wondered why she never extended herself. Just what dark secret held her at odds with the world and everyone in it?

We are only safe in our own heads.

On Friday, Steven boarded the 757, took his customary third row first class placement and settled in. He ordered a rum and coke, had the oysters Rockefeller and napped briefly. Fisher was feeling strong. He had the practice he had dreamt of and

21

money in the bank. There was no woman in his life but that was just how he liked to play. And this weekend, he really planned to play. Somehow even then he knew that something big was brewing. He could sense it, perhaps even smell it cooking. Steven would acquire something in Vegas that would change his life, even his perspective, forever. It did not come from a craps table or a slot machine. It was the prolific Las Vegas show.

Steven had rolled craps all day and surprisingly was up over three grand. Because he did not have an addiction to anything except power he never inebriated himself into any one victory. It was easy for him to release and stop while he was ahead. So on this evening, he headed for a show. Celine Dion was performing and while he could not stand to watch her sing, he did love to hear her sing. So he intended to close his eyes and just absorb the sound.

The opening act that evening was a hypnotist. His name was not memorable but everything else marked a permanent stain on Steven's brain. The hypnotist invited three audience members to the stage. The first man was a pastor who did not believe in hypnosis. The performer seemed to take great delight in the opportunity to belittle his belief. The second person was a grandmother of seven. She was more thrilled to be on stage than the hypnotist. The final participant was a blue collar worker from Detroit. He looked like he had played with a lot of cars from the permanent oil stain under his fingernails.

  The hypnotist started first with the pastor:

"So sir, you are a pastor?"

"Yes, indeed."

"And of what denomination?" he continued.

"I am an ordained Missionary Baptist Minister," the pastor proudly announced.

"So it is your job, is it not, to tell others about God?"

"That's the plan. HIS plan." The pastor then pointed to the heavens.

"What do you think about this movement today to take God out of public places?"

"All I can tell you is that God is alive and well and He will not be removed without a fight from the righteous," the pastor answered. As if to illustrate the power of the Cross, the minister held out both his arms at a 45-degree angle in crucifixion pose. A few members of the audience clapped at that. Steven never figured on Christians in Sin City. He was in fact shocked that this man was not laughed right off the stage.

 "That sounds great," the performer continued as he moved on to the grandmother. She was standing stage right in between the two men.

"Now, you said that you are a grandmother of seven, correct?"

The grandmother, stage struck and dumbfounded answered, "Yes, they are lovely, just lovely." She stared straight into the camera at the center of the stage giving her best deer in the headlights impression. She appeared to already be hypnotized.

"So have you ever done anything when you were younger that you would not want them to find out about?"

Grandma was all ears now. "What do you mean?"

"Oh, you know, did you ever do a strip tease or get drunk in public, or perhaps run around a bit?"

"I beg your pardon, young man. I will turn you over my knee," she threatened him. She was dead serious. The hypnotist took it in stride and made a face of faux fear pointed toward the audience.

They responded with massive patches of intermittent laughter that took some recovery time. He waited them out like any good performer knew to do and then declared:

"I'll take that as a 'no'."

But the laughter continued because the audience was on to him now. He moved on to the blue collar auto worker. The gentleman was in his early fifties but looked much younger. The hypnotist was most interested in this volunteer.

"Sir, can I ask you, how do you feel about being hypnotized tonight?"

"Don't have much for it."

"Then let's get it over with as soon as possible!" the performer responded.

"Sounds like a plan," the proud man responded.

The hypnotist just began talking. Steven noticed first the speed in which he spoke and the commanding tone of his voice. The Vegas performer did not seem to say anything out of the ordinary and even the audience was not aware that a hypnotism was taking place until he gave the three victims their assignments. Perhaps the real truth was that the audience had been hypnotized instead of the three on stage. Steven did often wonder if that was what had actually occurred.

The performer instructed the preacher to kneel and declare: "God is dead!" at the sound of a whistle. The hypnotist then blew a whistle hanging around his neck and the audience erupted in applause when the preacher knelt and yelled: "God is dead!"

He then told the pastor that there were lost souls in the building and he needed to go on a great commission and tell everyone that God is dead. The pastor immediately and quite passionately jumped to his feet and started running the aisles declaring to any and every one that God is dead. The audience was in hysterics.

He moved on to Grandma who had no expression on her face and told her that she was the best pole dancer in the world. He pointed to a pole that had been placed stage right and asked her to show everyone her moves. Gleefully she mounted the silver obelisk, raised her day dress and began to slide and writhe herself upon the chrome. She placed her finger in her mouth and slowly moved it down her body. The audience was gasping for air. Granny rode the pole like a pro.

He approached the auto worker but before he could say one word the man declared:

"That weren't right what you did. That is a man of God and you will reap what you just sowed. And what you did to that poor little granny.....you oughtern be ashamed of yourself."

 The man exited the stage and the building.

Unshaken, the hypnotist simply stated: "You can't get them all."

Steven's Exodus

Dr. Fisher rolled the hypnotist act around and around in his mind. He could not release the thought of the amount of control one human had displayed over another and it was consuming him.

"Could I get you another beverage? It will be the last service before we land in New York," the flight attendant interrupted his thinking.

"No, but thank you," Steven responded. The attendant nodded in agreement and headed to the next aisle to interrogate the guy in 5B.

*If I could be taught the mechanics of hypnotism, how to do what I saw him do, it might double my current practice. I could use it for good, to help cure patients of their weaknesses. I could eliminate anxieties, alcoholism, drug addictions and gambling ...*but his mind stopped him there.

He had just left Las Vegas, carelessness incorporated. He knew that he was risking his future, the stakes were incredibly high and the odds unbettable. But it didn't matter how many lies he whispered to himself or even how good those fallacies were, his inner voice enunciated with much higher volume.

First, do no harm.

The doctor's spoken oath.

But Dr. Steven F. Fisher never listened to that voice.

The Doctor Is In

Calliope's face ghostens as she swings open the door to the medical complex. *Alcohol*, she thinks. *Alcohol and old blood-that's what this place always smells like.* She knows that the janitorial staff tries to mask the odor, but they are rarely successful.

Calliope approaches the elevator, presses the up arrow and patiently waits. Her anxiety level is average today, not too high, not that low. Ding. It is here. She enters the cubicle and allows it to rise her to the floor she selects, four. Ding. She exits the tiny box, looks up to the sign on the wall and follows its directions taking a sharp left, then another and stopping at the door of: Dr. Steven Francis Fisher, Psychotherapist.

"Hmmm," she says. Out loud. To no one. She taps lightly almost hoping he will not hear.

"Come in, please," is the female response.

She turns the long, twisted, silver handle and enters. Seated at the desk is a mildly attractive 23-year-old with red reading glasses sliding down her nose, typing silently on the lap top to her left. Madame Secretary turns, immediately makes an assessment based on Calliope's appearance and then whines,

"May I help you?"

"I have an appointment, Calliope Cash." Three heads in the waiting room shoot up.

"With Dr. Fisher?"

28

No, idiot, with Dr. Seuss.

"Yes, ma'am."

"I'm younger than you, there is no need for the formality," snippy returns.

"How would you know if you are younger than me?" Calliope pops back.

"I am Dr. Fisher's executive secretary. I know everything."

"Well, I guess THAT is good to know. When can I expect to be seen?"

"Shortly, take a seat."

Calliope selects a soft couch fuming inside at the rude exchange, the invasion of her privacy and the unwritten rule that a doctor's time is infinitely more important than anyone else's. She is also stewing on the words she wishes she had said......

Calliope reaches into her Luis Vitton bag, retrieves a book of short stories by Breece D 'J Pancake and immerses herself into a more engaging situation. The door to the office opens once again and a small, weasely man enters the room. He is short in stature and screams Joe Pesci. He holds a cell phone to his ear with one hand and is gesturing with the other as if the recipient can see each expression. The digits move in unison for it would seem he needs his whole palm to make his point. Shortly after entering, he kills the call and returns the device to his left front pocket. Weasel quickly scans the entire area and his frantic gaze pauses on Calliope. It stays just a moment too long.

I KNOW her. Victoria's Secret.

Calliope feels the intensity of an almost dripping stare.

Great, now the psychos are arriving!

Weasel checks in with Madame Secretary and takes a seat perpendicular to Calliope. She feels his eyes on her but she is experienced at ignoring the attention. Weasel asks if there is a public restroom. The secretary points to a door at the front of the office. Weasel enters and Calliope hears the distinct sound of recycled Pepsi.

At least it isn't alongside the more disgusting song of self-exploration. Gag me. He has to know we can HEAR that!

The door coasts open once again and in swirl a middle-aged mother dragging her five-year-old offspring. The small child is digging in her tender heels and resisting her capture. Mother is relentless and determined. The smaller female is wearing a large and lacy bow adorning a ponytail pulled so tight the child is turning Asian before her very eyes.

Oh my God! A lacy bow sends the same message as a leisure suit. Clearly, you are not on top of the trends.

It irritates Calliope even more that the child's outfit is definitely top dog. No Walmart here. Calliope Cash can be unforgiving when it comes to fashion in the same way a dentist cannot conceive of someone who does not floss. She, herself, has been immersed in the fashion scene since her nineteenth year. Literally immersed, she adorns catwalks in Milan and New York and is considered a permanent fixture of fashion week. This very profession is what compels her to this complex. Bulimia is her secret battlefield and Cee Cee has heard through the grapevine that the good doctor treats several of her friends for the same affliction. And with great success. She is hoping for the same results as her career is so accelerated that she does not get enough privacy to vomit. And she is starting to look a little worse for the wear with the hint of dark circles and the faintest sign of sunken cheeks. This simply cannot happen. Her face has an estimated worth and she holds the policy to prove it. Calliope is top dollar. This she knows. She cannot help but know it.

Weasel completes his dirty business and exits the rest room. He tries to appear nonchalant as he chooses a seat closer to Calliope than his previous placement despite many vacancies elsewhere. Calliope ruses a minor adjustment in her outfit and uses the opportunity to move three inches away from him.

Idiot thinks I don't remember he first took a seat over there!

But, again, she is accustomed to this behavior and so she again ignores it.

"Mommy, is mean doctor going to stick me with a needle?" the small female child inquires.

"No, baby, not today. This is a different kind of doctor. He is just going to ask you questions," her mother responds.

"What kind of questions?" she continues.

 "Oh, honey it is nothing to get nervous about. He wants you to tell him about daddy," the mother responds, her deep Southern drawl dropping syllables like thick honey.

"What about daddy?" the child persists.

The mother looks about the room and discovers a very interested weasel and a mortified model. She makes a quick assessment.

"Sissy girl, let's cover this later, how's that? And then maybe top it with some ice cream?" Her southern drawl misspells cream to crame as it erupts from her mouth.

The child claps her hands excitedly and screams: "Yes, yes, yes, with shrinkles!" "Anything you want lovey dove," rich mom responds.

Wow, I must be witnessing the parent of the year. Let us drag our child kicking and screaming to a shrink discussing how horrible her daddy is in front of strangers and then bribe her with a dairy product! I am never having children!

Calliope knows she has no real choice in the matter. Her career is too accelerated to take nine months off and then there is "The Incident." Motherhood is just not in her cards. And where would she even put a baby? Despite her success, her New York apartment is the size of a small garage and at some point, the closets are full.

Calliope glances once again at Dr. Fisher's secretary who is on the phone with some client arranging an appointment.

She monitors her silver Omega checking the time, sighs and begins to think on Jeff, the one thing she can't give up. He is not who everyone expects her to love: he is as far from the industry as one could get. Jeff works as a technician for a large communications company. They met on a set shoot. While she struts 30-foot stages that go nowhere he ascends 500 foot towers so cell phones will work when they need to work. He is a good guy, and she had even recently confessed to him:

"I am so glad that God gave you to me and if He is not responsible, then I am glad that I took you by force."

Calliope and Jeff secretly eloped. It is a sticking point with him and they have managed to keep it quiet now for almost two years but Calliope is resistant to admitting the marriage. She is not at all embarrassed of the relationship, just wise enough to realize a single model sells better. And she knows eventually they will be found out because'those dirt bags search records everywhere and pay off civil servants for information. For now, they put the issue to bed as each is content to be with the other. In the two years since they wed, Jeff and Calliope have only shared the same air for about 5 months total. Mrs. Seaton never goes by Mrs. Seaton and is careful to not write Jeff's name on anything. Not the lease. Not the car. Not even the hotel rooms where they check in separately. She erases his name from her life but only because she loves him that much. It is private. It is just hers. And it is easy to do because Jeff travels as much as Calliope. Their reunions are glorious hours of love and sexual calisthentics. That ketchup song really is true: anticipation…

Calliope closes her eyes for a bit and relives their morning romp. She loves the way Jeff is so spontaneous and sweet when courting her affections. This morning after her shower, she slipped on a tiny American Eagle shirt, and pulled it snugly over the girls. She stepped into the hall and Jeff immediately responded:

"Woman, when you come out like that and your headlights are on….I just want to….uhhhhhh….." his response is more primal than verbal.

Coyly, Calliope returned, "You just want to what?"

"I just want to lay a wet one right on them," he finished.

"Go ahead, the girls are waiting," Calliope teased as she lifted her t-shirt exposing two perfectly perky and natural specimens. Her "girls" defied gravity. Jeff leaned in and lightly caressed one nipple, then the next, gently with his lips.

Calliope responded physically and then verbally, "Now this girl (indicating her left breast) thinks you kissed that girl too long and she is a bit jealous about it."

34

"Oh, I so sorry," he baby talked her. "I fix that right away," and he completed the same action in reverse lingering longer on the left breast than the right one this time.

Calliope loved it when he baby talked her.

 "Now it's even. See ya' down the hall," she answered as she scooted toward their bedroom.

"It's a date!"

 Calliope wades in the morning memory glowing inside and out from the love she feels for this man.

 He has not wilted to her impeccable beauty, he has responded to, fallen in love with, and hunted her heart. That is why he has won it.

And then Calliope thinks about something else.

 It is something altogether evil she places in the back of her brain visiting only when it is otherwise unavoidable. She goes there on rare occasions to assess its significance. For Calliope tucks the whole ugly mess safely in the past, to some finite lobe because she is determined not to be scarred by it. But, just like breakfast, it comes back up.

Second History Lesson

The Incident

The day began like any other day. It was warm and
Calliope was running way ahead of schedule. She
argued briefly with her sister not knowing then that
those arguments would be the longest conversations
they would ever have. Calliope and her sister had
parallel lives and there were many things that should
have connected them on common ground. But then,
as is now, they simply had nothing to say to each
other. Perhaps they were not compatible. Or maybe
the only thing they had in common was the womb
they shared. It may have been jealousy. Calliope was
stunning as a child, teen and adult and Ann could not
handle that. Calliope often paid the price for her DNA.
Pretty ain't all fun and games and the price can run
steep.

 The real truth was that neither girl cared enough
about the other to explore the reasons. They just left
it there.

"You are going to be late for your shoot!" the girls'
mother yelled upstairs.

 "I am ready," Calliope screamed as she descended.

Her mother handed her a granola bar and a protein
shake and tossed the keys to the Jeep across the
counter. "Fill it up on the way back, ok?"

"Not a prob!" Calliope responded.

"Good luck, Cee Cee. I hope you get some great
shots!"

"Thanks, Mama. See you in a couple hours or less," Calliope said as she blew a kiss across the kitchen.

 Calliope's Christian name was Calliope Grace Carmichael. It was pure coincidence that three years later Ford modeling agency had it changed to another surname with the letter "C" thereby protecting her nickname of Cee Cee. They called her Cash and laughed about it. They knew exactly, even at the ripe old age of 18, what they had. A cash cow. So they called her what she was and smiled as the checks rolled in.

Calliope opened the front door of their modest family home and skipped lightly to the Jeep. She opened the unlocked door and hopped up into the seat, turned the key in the ignition and rolled her eyes when it traveled too far on the steering column.

 "Crap, I need that fixed."

She pulled up and out of the inclined driveway, turned right, then left and right again onto I-75 heading into town. She decided to stop at a gas station on the way to her appointment as she was still an hour ahead of schedule. She pulled into the Exxon at the end of I-75 where it meets Route 52. Exiting the Jeep, she corrected her lipstick in the window with one hand while she pumped premium with the other.

Calliope completed her gas purchase, re-entered her Jeep and headed north on Highway 52 into town. Calliope arrived at Hensley Photo Studios and entered the building. She didn't notice the three men in the truck watching her, never looking their way.

"Hey, Chip," Calliope tossed the photographer.

"Howdy doo perty girl. You 'bout ready to throw down some gorgeous?" Chip returned.

"Why not? It's either that or clean my room-and everyone knows that's not happening!" Calliope loved to tease him. He was fun.

"Okay, girlie, head to the dressing room. Sis has some things lined out for today," Chip instructed.

"OK. Back in a flash, Gordon!" Chip chuckled at Calliope's exchange.

He liked this girl. He didn't want her. He just liked her. That made all the difference. And he sensed deep within that she was special. She had genuine charisma, a real gravitational pull.

Calliope and Chip worked for 17 minutes on head shots before the camera jammed. "Crap! Cee Cee, I have to fix this. Let's reschedule for early next week, ok?"

"Not a prob! See ya' then buttercup!"

"Real deal, Steel! Sorry for the delay!" Chip replied. Calliope returned to Sis who helped her back into her street attire and then headed for the Jeep.

Calliope left feeling unsatisfied at the session and anxious about the quality of the proofs and her overall portfolio. She entered the Jeep, once again unlocked, and placed the key in the ignition. And once again the key drifted too far on the steering column.

"Do not scream," the faceless voice instructed her.

Was that in my head?

"Uh, what?"

"I said, do not scream. Do not look in the back seat, I won't hurt you. I just need a ride out of here. Drive me to the flood wall near 7th street and I will get out and leave you alone," the voice continued.

Calliope's fear was forming tornadoes in her throat and she thought instantly of jumping from the car and running up the sidewalk. But there was a calmness to his cadence that told her he would honor his word. And fear had crippled her ability to reason this correctly.

"Ok." And so she did.

During the short drive, Calliope tried to steal glances of the voice in the back seat by peeking in the rear view mirror. She could not see him, her abductor had sunk down beneath the height of the car window.

   When she arrived at the flood wall, she took little notice of the white utility truck parked just inside the barrier. She was more concerned with the faceless entity in the back seat.

"Pull near the rest rooms, put the car in park and set the emergency brake," the back seat told her. She did as she was told.

"Now, enter the women's restroom, wait ten minutes and then you can leave."

"Ok, thanks." *Did I just thank the man who kidnapped me?*

Calliope quickly left the Jeep intentionally abandoning her beloved Coach bag on the front seat hoping it would sweeten the deal and he would actually allow her to go. She gently pushed open the restroom door and stepped in. Carefully she listened for the screech of the engine convinced her new friend was intent on stealing her vehicle. Instead, she heard the door open again. Three men stepped into the women's restroom with Calliope. Each man was big but not in the good way and one was standing closer to Calliope than the others. She spoke to this man.

"Can I help you?"

"Yes, I am sure you can," he answered.

"I'm not sure that I understand....."

"I think you probably do," he returned. It was not a sinister statement. It was matter of fact. And that made it more terrifying. He sounded more like a late night disc jockey, velvety and smooth. She heard it in her head.

And now for our great visual pleasure, we shall take you, absolutely all of you. What a weird sentence to imagine pre-rape.

Calliope's eyes moved from one man to the next.

She scanned each incredible specimen and then announced: "Ok, so I always said that if this ever happened to me that I would just give you the best lay of your life so you would let me go after it was over. How does that sound to you?"

Calliope saw no need to mention that she had no clue what that was. These three would be her first. There is no coming back from that-it is unforgettable, infinite and permanent damage. It shows up forever.

The three men never answered or even showed their amusement about her strategy-they simply took her. They took every inch of her in the very worst way a young woman can be taken in the floor of a filthy public restroom. One at a time and two at a time they took her pounding away at every cell that comprised her being. And then they left her on the cold, urine-stained floor in a pile of scarlet flesh. In a pool of menstrual blood. It made their dirty deed, nasty.

And then a voice, like conscience, whispered.

He does not defile his neighbor's wife or lie with a woman during her period. Ezekiel 18:6

They reached deep down and pulled all the ME, out of me.

Calliope scrapes off the scar with the sound of Madame Secretary's: "Dr. Fisher will see you now."

Quickly, she brushes imaginary crumbs from the folds of her Michael Kors skirt, rises and follows the secretary's pointed finger to an office behind the appointment desk. She enters, and is overawed at the décor. It is not spectacular or showy, just elegant. A modest crystal chandelier is suspended between a couch and the doctor's hickory desk. The furniture is eclectic as if each piece has been hand-selected to sit where it is. There are various statues placed on small tables scattered around the room. The doctor is writing with a two-hundred-dollar pen and when she shakes his hand she likens it to squishing satin.

She asks, "Where should I be?"

"Anywhere you would like," the good doctor returns.

Calliope chooses a straight-back IKEA number, comfortable and modern. She takes a moment to peruse the art work adorning the office walls. She recognizes Pollock and Monet, an odd combination she thinks, and wonders if they are originals. They most certainly could be based on the other decor.

"I am Dr. Fisher. Could I interest you in a soft drink or some confection?" Calliope nods no.

"I'm good," she answers him.

"What have you come to see me about today?" *All business, he is.*

"Geez, you just jump right in, don't you?" Calliope responds.

"I'm too expensive for small talk." He seems proud to announce this.

Cannot believe you admitted that!

Calliope pauses and studies the good doctor's face. He looks harmless enough.

"How about a little conversation first? Clearly I will cover some sensitive issues but I don't like this ambushed feeling. It's too callous." Calliope lives for distraction.

"OK, let us play. Tell me about your childhood."
Steven likes this game.

"Best ever. Grew up in a large subdivision with 257
homes and a community pool. The pool was the heart
of the community. I spent ninety percent of every
summer in that chemical pond. If I close my eyes, I
can still smell the chlorine and taste liquid Snickers I
purchased from the concession stand. Of course the
lady at the concession stand always froze the
Snickers but let's be real, shall we? Not even a dog
can penetrate the first bite of a frozen Snickers so I
tossed those candy bricks with caramel mortar onto
beach towels depicting fish, sand and sea shells until
pool break while the sun slowly morphed them into
the terry cloth fibers. I always tried to rescue the
remnant from its wilted wrapper." Calliope continues
on but Steven is no longer listening, he is assessing
her.

Steven is overwhelmingly impressed with Calliope's
storytelling prowess. He also recognizes the
camouflage. She is attempting to impress him with
her personality. Probably wants me to like her and
not the image of her. He is intrigued. Because he
cannot escape his training, he also suspects Attention
Deficit Disorder. It amuses him how quickly she
transitions from a pool to a melted Snickers bar. It
makes him feel powerful to diagnose so quickly. Of
course, he assumes his own accuracy on the matter.

"Ok, what else? How did you do in school?" Steven
presses her.

"Well, I know enough about how things work to understand that the world needs me to be stupid so they can conclude that a modeling career was my only option, but I graduated in the top tenth of my class. I aspired to be an attorney and I wanted to work in criminal defense."

But that was before the bathroom floor fiasco.

A head hunter showed up on my tiny little hometown campus and the rest is history. From sophomore to Vogue in two sentences.

"And your parents? Normal childhood?" he continues.

"Mom and Dad were Ozzie and Harriet. They never let me party, be a cheerleader or date without a chaperone. I never got into any real trouble on my own accord." Calliope studies the floor.

"What does that mean? Did you get into trouble at someone else's beckoning?" Now she has Steven's full attention.

"Kinda', but it wasn't my fault. That is not a first date discussion, though." Calliope shuts it down.

"Are we dating, Calliope?" Steven feels his heart rate soaring.

This woman is having quite an effect on him and it makes him simultaneously excited and uncomfortable. Steven does not usually respond this way to women.

These words rush through him faster than the blood heading south.

Calliope, pensive, replies," It is kind of like dating. I show up at a specified day and time that we agree to in advance. You offer me a snack or a beverage. We talk about personal stuff. You fix me. Sounds like a relationship to me."

Calliope knows in this moment she will definitely tell him about the incident but never about her marriage. There is a small piece of her that still enjoys a good teaser. And Calliope likes to keep the beautiful parts private.

"That is not very professional on my part." Steven did not care at all about being professional but he will never give the appearance of such impropriety.

"Professional smessional. This is our little game and we can make up the rules as we go. Are you in or not?" Calliope raises her eyebrows and lets her face ask the question.

Oh, I am all in!

Reasonable thinking would suggest that he pull back just a bit, it is too early to set the hook. Steven needs to establish trust with her. Perhaps, in this instance, she is fishing for him and he is amazed at how much he wants this. Steven glances at his Rolex and discovers Calliope has only been in his office for fifteen minutes. Steven overlooks Calliope's query and poses his own:

"Has anyone in your family ever been exposed to hypnosis before? Or have they sought help in this particular area of therapy?" Dr. Fisher is attempting to recover a professional rapport. The erection in his designer pants is objecting at the moment.

"Not that I am aware of, but it is not like we ever had a discussion about hypnotism or even bulimia for that matter," Calliope answers him.

"So I take it you are indeed bulimic?" Steven presses on.

"Well, I have been too ashamed to get a proper diagnosis, but I make myself throw up almost every meal. Except breakfast. I never vomit breakfast. I like it too much." Calliope is looking at the floor to keep herself from losing control.

"What do you typically have for breakfast?"

"Strawberry Pop Tarts. Frosted. They are the best." And she licked her lips to prove it.

You are doing that on purpose, Steven imagines.

"Miss Cash, I am treating several others in your profession with eating disorders. I have had some success in managing bulimia but it is truly contingent on your desire to rid yourself of this obsession. I don't want to make any promises, but I would like to work with you and see just where it might go." Steven returns to his professional demeanor.

And I know where I want it to go, pretty little girl.

"Let's just finish this for today. This is an introductory appointment. I have fully read your questionnaire so I am briefed on where our sessions may be headed. Let me reflect on the things you have told me and schedule another session on your way out for next

Tuesday at four. Plan to stay longer at the next session."

 He has not even scratched the surface of her need to see him but he also knows that she is not ready to reveal anything just yet. Steven wonders to himself how long it will be before she elaborates on her eating disorder but he willingly dances her little sidestep.

I will break the bricks in that wall.

"Oh, Ok. You are at least efficient. I thought we had more time…." Calliope trails off.

 Dr. Fisher appears calm but his heart rate is off the chart and he is in a predicament that requires him to remain seated as Calliope exits the room.

Calliope pauses at the doorway, looks over her left shoulder and says: "By the way, your clerk out here is a bit big for her britches, don't you think?"

"It's hard to get good help," he wavers away. Inside, he is amused and bewildered by this incredible creature who has no inhibitions, no filter and no guard up. He fantasizes about the possibilities. He is definitely in the game, her game, because he has seen some semblance of this before: too familiar and ingratiating. He also knows it is her unparalleled beauty that has him. And he is had.

Third History Lesson

Tommy Untied

Vinnie stumbles backwards, spiraling into a steel beam. Tommy, pulpy and oozing, sees an opportunity with his unswelled eye to wriggle from his zip tie bondage. As the Weasel faces the wall huffing and trying to regain his balance, Tommy frees his hands. Because the adrenaline surging within Tommy is more powerful than his recent memory, he forgets that his legs have been butchered and he instantly eats concrete. The seriousness of Tommy's potential escape, not lost on Vinnie, forces him into immediate action. The adrenaline in Vinnie is also alive and well. Vinnie reaches into his left sock, unsheathes the stiletto housed there, then swiftly and proficiently uses Tommy's throat to separate his head from the rest of him. Tommy gagged, hacked, sputtered and bled profusely before sliding to the floor in a twisted, broken, pathetic heap.

"That was a close one," Vinnie gasps as he seals his contractual obligation.

 Poor Vinnie is off his game. Something has to be done and this good doctor is his best option. Of course Vinnie knows that he will eventually need to assassinate Dr. Fisher when the sessions are completed, which is also just business, and he plans to wait until he is sure that this hypnotherapy crap is working. Vinnie doesn't want his name to be on someone else's work order. Dr. Fisher is only vaguely aware of the danger that shares air with him each appointment.

The more hits I have under me, the odds are my name shows up on someone else's job.

Vinnie hears the office door move to open and looks up to see his supermodel reappear. (*Thanks for the memories!*) He chuckles a bit thinking his restroom rendezvous is his little secret; he had wanted to yank his sausage but quickly decided against it. He wasn't sure how thick the walls were in the office and he didn't want an audience. The disgusted look on Calliope's face makes him briefly question whether she could read his thoughts.

Hey, now, Miss High and Mighty. At least I don't make my living in a fake bedroom, half-clothed looking all lusty while sucking on the same finger in every shot.

Vinnie despises judgment. He knows what his will be, any good Catholic knows.

"Mr. Castana, the doctor will see you now," Honeycut announces.

What an annoying whine you have my pretty.

He ponders briefly about this weird little woman and considers her mean. Not California "Mean Girls" mean per say, but he imagines she is the type who likes to flick bees out of flowers. Vinnie rises and limps toward the door, arthritis has crippled his ability to retreat. He doesn't ask where he should sit but instead scans the room for the chair or couch with the highest cushion-a necessary assessment given the status of his joints. Vinnie is accustomed to sitting wherever he chooses. He selects a love seat adjacent to the doctor's desk and settles into it.

"Mr. Castana, I am Dr. Fisher. I specialize in hypnotherapy and I understand from my secretary that you have been experiencing some anxiety, is that correct?" Jumping in with personal history questions too quickly with Calliope forces Fisher to switch his strategy a bit.

"Hold youse horses, Doc. Let's establish some ground rules. Everything I give youse, youse can't give it up to no one, right?" Not even the Feds?"

"Mr. Castana, confidentiality is a serious matter with this office and you are free to speak about any aspect of your life to me. It will be best if you are completely honest so that my assessment and diagnosis will determine the best medical help for you," Dr. Fisher returns.

"Ok, so how do youse think youse would hold up under torture?" Vinnie cocks his head to one side and awaits the doctor's answer.

Dr. Fisher pauses briefly and then replies:

 "That is probably anyone's guess. How could you know if you have not been through it? I imagine it would be like war-you know how you hope you will react but you still might pile up like a four-year-old and cry for your mommy." Steven appears satisfied.

"I see youse point, Doc." Vinnie pauses as if assessing the good doctor's reliability. He continues,

"Well, I have been having little episodes and I can't seem to get them in line." Vinnie actually looks embarrassed.

"Does your heart race?" Dr. Fisher presses.

"Yea, it's like a marathon in my chest!" Vinnie answers.

"Do you have excessive perspiration?" the doctor queries.

"Excessive what?" Vinnie returns.

"Perspiration, do you sweat?" Dr. Fisher explains.

"Oh, yah, yah like a whore in church." Then Vinnie chuckles, responding to his own declaration.

"Hmmm. Have you noticed any particular pattern in these attacks? For instance, are they occurring in the mornings or just after a certain beverage or any other characteristic that might be a common denominator?" Steven is proficient with his interrogation.

"Now that youse mention it, I only seem to have one when I am on a job, youse know, under contract," Vinnie reveals.

"Well, job stress is a common trigger for mild panic attacks. Deadlines and projections can wreak havoc on a body's chemistry." Steven offers.

"That explains it, Doc. I never could do Chemistry. Huh, huh." Vinnie chuckles again, amusing only himself.

Dr. Fisher ignores the comment and continues,

"Do you have any extracurricular activities that help you wash off your day?"

"Nah. I stay on call 24/7. If the boss needs me, I'm available." Vinnie offers.

"Well, it might be more connected to the actual work rather than the long hours. What are your job specifications?" Steven asks.

Suspicious now, Vinnie questions,

"Is youse wired?"

"Excuse me?" Steven raises both brows, incredulous at the accusation.

"I'll take that as a 'no', 'cause if youse is, youse have to say youse is," Vinnie replies.

"Mr. Castana, I am interested in trying to help you but I get the feeling I am in the middle of The Godfather. Am I at any risk if I treat you?" Steven looks a bit nervous.

"Nah, nah Doc, youse fine. I need help. My boss can't use me if I can't work and muscle men don't retire, they sink." Vinnie likes knowing more about something than the good doctor does.

The doctor understands the reference perfectly. At last, he has some inkling of what he is up against.

You're Getting Sleepy..Sleepy…

Steven sits behind an elegant desk reading from a medical journal:

The induction of hypnosis is frequently used to place a person into a state of trance.   This state is robot-like, yet not robotic. The entranced individual is capable of acting and reacting to normal stimuli. The subject may or may not remember all or part of their experience while under the hypnotic trance.

Ha! I worked that one out for you! My patients don't remember squat!

He continues reading from the journal.

When administering hypnosis, direct the subject to lie down and stare at an object. Instruct the subject to take deep breaths……

Impatiently, Steven flips through the pages searching for a particular topic. He finds it quickly:

Post Hypnotic Suggestion and The Consequences.

And Steven digs in.

Peyton Jane's Brain

Peyton rises early even though her husband, Brad, is out of town. She wipes the night from her face and staggers into the kitchen. She opens the cabinet over the stovetop and retrieves the Folger's coffee. Pausing, she returns it to its rightful spot and instead reaches deeper into the cabinet for the remnant of Starbucks Breakfast Blend residing in its almost depleted bag. She puts the coffee on, grabs a lemon yogurt and sidles into the family room of her mid-entry house. She sits in "her" chair and attempts to ignore the Iphone beckoning her attention. PJ lasts all of 43 seconds before she sets the yogurt on the end table, codes in with her fingerprint and presses the Facebook button. She tries to fool herself into believing she is just scrolling anyone when his post pops up. PJ tries not to comment but immediately she knows something clever she wants to say and more importantly she wants to see how long it takes him to LIKE her comment of his MEME. So she comments:

"What a brave post!" to his image of an American Indian in full headdress with the caption:

Our Next Commander in Chief

Within three seconds he likes it. She determines it means that he also likes her. This is only happening in her brain and even she is aware enough to know it. Now, like a snowball rolling downhill, it is growing and escalating and she is attaching too much meaning to his every post. His every meme. His every everything.

Instead of continuing, she rubs ashes on her forehead and signs out.

I am cursed. Am I too bold to think it is me he loves? All I can think about is seeing him eye to eye, and then figuring it out. Oh, I am treading in dangerous water here. I will know when I see him. His eyes piercing mine. His soul piercing mine. His heart piercing mine.

How did one day do this? The simple incomplete passage of one day. I am posting my unfailing love for Brad on Thursday and numb to the sentiment by Friday mid-morning. Stalking another man's profile, even.

Why? Is my foundation so unsturdy, so weakened, that a boy I barely knew, barely KNOW, can crumble it in under 50 words? And if it is, explain the longevity of my marriage. Just when did this happen?

He has nothing to offer me but his brilliance. And I know that I would worship at his feet, a sin much greater than others. Just how could I even reason that out? I would have to do it. He has already won me with his words. I know exactly what mistake I am making and my mind is still deliberately choosing to go there. What the hell is wrong with me? My heart races at the thought and I am having sexual fantasies that I have not thought of in years. I am too excited about the possibility of this, this unrequited seduction of my very soul. My eternity.

I need help.

Above all, I need prayer.

Then Peyton Jane stares intensely at her phone almost willing Dr. Fisher to ring it.

EXODUS

Sessions: Mother of the Year

"The doctor will see you now."

Mother of the year and her wiry offspring remove themselves from a tan leather love seat and walk in to the doctor's office.

"Please take any seat." Mom and daughter select a couch directly across from Dr. Fisher.

Dr. Fisher continues, "Now, Mrs. Marcum, you were a bit vague in your information sheet so I will need you to tell me exactly why you have brought young Isabel to see me today. And, if this is a difficult conversation, then we can excuse Isabel to the next room where there are some diversions she may enjoy."

"Thank you, Doctor, but that won't be necessary. She brought her Game Boy and she will not be in any way interested in what you and I have to discuss," her slow Southern superior drawl annoying the doctor with every twangy syllable.

Go South. Go home. Do it now.

"If you insist. Very well. Let's begin. Why have you come to see a hypnotherapist today, and more specifically, why me?" Dr. Fisher inquires.

"Well, it is a little delicate. I was reading all about your practice in the Time Magazine article and I was intrigued. I came here because I have had a very troubled marriage and poor Isabel has suffered immensely at the hands of my soon-to-be ex-husband."

"Was he physically or emotionally abusive to her?" Dr. Fisher presses her.

"Not exactly, but that is what I want to inquire about," Mrs. Marcum declares.

"I am not sure that I am following you." Steven appears to be confused.

"This is so embarrassing. My husband works on Wall Street. We are a family of great means and my beloved decided to enter into an illicit affair with his secretary."

Isabel comes to life. "Mommy, what does lissit mean?"

"It means happy, sweetie. Play your game." Steven could see how easily this Southern matriarch was able to lie to her child. He tucks that piece of information away for later.

"Okey dokey." Isabel sings back. Southern Mother continues her tale.

"This woman he is seeing is not of good character and I will not allow Isabel to be around her." She makes the announcement as if there is no other feasible alternative.

"Mrs. Marcum that sounds like a decision that a judge should make, not me," Dr. Fisher responds.

Southern Mother reacts like a wounded animal, screaming: "A judge does not know my daughter and her needs the way that I know my daughter and her needs!"

"What exactly is it that you want from me in this particular situation?" the confused physician asks her.

"Well, you see, I thought that maybe, if you could just plant a tiny little white trash memory into Isabel's recollection then she could relate that to a caseworker and the whole custody inconvenience would be a moot point," she holds her stare, unmoving, refined and precise.

"You're not serious." But Steven already knows she is.

Mrs. Marcum shuffles her feet and ruffles the sleeves on her expensive blouse and answers:

"Indeed I am," she confirms.

Dr. Fisher takes a slow inward breath and calmly states: "I want you to stand and immediately walk out of this office. Do not say one more word to me."

Mrs. Marcum stands to her feet, slides her right hand across the tight bun of her hair, calls to her child and strolls from the office with her head held high.

Wow, the nerve.

Steven presses the call button on the intercom. Bzzz.

"Yes, Dr. Fisher?" Honeycut returns.

"Miss Honeycut, I need you to pull the tape from the last session and transpose it as soon as possible. File the original and send a copy immediately to my attorney, George. I will dictate a cover letter later."

"As you wish," Honeycut replies.

*Every time she says that I think of <u>Princess Bride</u>.
And how dare that little Southern bitch try to
manipulate me. The whole deal stinks of entrapment.*

Steven, inherently cold, unsympathetic and well,
downright evil does not necessarily object to the
notion of planting those ideas in young Isabel's mind.
If fact, he rather responds to the implication. What he
cannot handle, what he simply will not accept is, that
it is not HIS idea.

Steven sits back in his leather chair and tries to
repress the thoughts running rampant. It is of no use.
Marcum has sparked him. If he can plant her ideas,
he can plant his as well.

Vinnie's Exodus

Vinnie stumbles out of the medical complex and begins walking parallel to the busy city street. A black Oldsmobile pulls beside him as he sidles down the sidewalk. A window rolls down. Vinnie turns his head just in time to see Nick and Carmine seated in the front, eyeballing his every move.

"Boss called you up," Nick tells him

"What......now?!" Vinnie exclaims.

"We wouldn't be here if he meant tomorrow. Get the fuuuhh..... (stopping in mid curse) in."

The other guys know not to throw down foul in front of Vinnie.

"Fellas, what's this about?" Carmine answers him. "How the heck should we know? Boss says: Get Vinnie, we get Vinnie."

Nick adds: "It's something about that job on Tommy. I don't got no more details."

Oh crap! How did he find out? I am done.

It is all Vinnie can do to maintain control at this point.

"Take me to him," Vinnie returns.

"That is the plan," Carmine replies.

Vinnie opens the door to enter the vehicle and slowly, creaking from his knees, sits down. He scoots himself to the middle. And then he feels it creeping up from within.

*No, no, no, NO! Calm youself. It's happening, it's
happening! Slow down blood, heart hold youse
horses. Not now, not now, NOT NOW!!!!!*

The palpitations take off. His heart rate is sky
rocketing to an unsurvivable number. Vinnie slides left
in the back seat of the Olds, a red traffic light
streaking and coloring his descent.
 His next thought is of fresh water spilling over shades
of grey smacking loudly on rocks. He hears the creek
so vividly, it is almost like he is right there, on the
bank, dipping his toes in the water. The fiery streak
running through his cheek forces him to realize that
Nick is slapping him back to consciousness.

"Vinnie! Vinnie! Is you dead or something?"

"Not yet, but if you don't stop smacking me, YOUSE
will be soon!" Vinnie retorts.

Now Vinnie is not the kind of guy to hold a grudge, so
he lets the smacking go. Nicky is scared and just
trying to help, besides Vinnie is currently more
concerned about the meeting than his personal
embarrassment. But Vinnie will let you in on all that
later.

Calliope's Exodus

On the short drive to her apartment, Calliope, as she often does, re-enacts every word she and the good Dr. Fisher exchanged. She often even alters the dialogue. Was I too flirtatious? Calliope experiences true remorse when she uses her assets for evil.

If he cannot help me control my desire to toss every cookie I consume, I am in real trouble. I have a time constraint here. And I have to be ready to deliver. The Hypothesis Jeans shoot is on the docket and I have committed to do the campaign.

Calliope makes a quick mirror assessment and decides she looks passable. She repairs the color on her lips and smacks them against each other. She has no idea why she does, it is something her mother has taught her. Despite her impeccable face, Cee Cee does not place much value on appearance. She hangs around the house sans decoration of any kind except a bit of lip gloss and prefers an almost destroyed pair of sweat pants to any designer dud she has donned to date. Although her life might be considered glamorous to some, her mind is where it should be. She holds up her end for her employer and goes here and there to protect the image they give her (along with that stupid surname) but she never sells out to it. She loves her husband and is doing whatever she can now to protect what they hope to one day have. Anonymity.

 Calliope calls Jeff on her cell and asks him to meet her at Fab Patty's for dinner.   Calliope contacts the restaurant's manager, Fred, and arranges for her usual private setting in the back where no one knows a table even exists. She walks toward the hall tree and grabs Jeff's extra-large, grey hoodie and puts it on. She pulls the hood way up and over her hair and finds a massive pair of Gucci sunglasses, modeling them in the mirror.

"That ought to do it," she exclaims out loud to no one but herself.

Jeff powers off his cell phone and does a quick mirror assessment. He brushes down his eyebrows and checks for straggler lunch between his teeth. He reaches into the console of his 2009 Ford F-150 and retrieves a Breath Saver mint, wintergreen.

"Might just get me some sugar today," he exclaims out loud to no one but himself.

Jeff runs as quickly after Calliope as she does him. It feels good to be so mutually enamored of someone. Neither one takes those blessings for granted. Calliope arrives at Fab Patty's first, undetected, and is rapidly ushered to her private oasis. Jeff arrives two minutes after Cee Cee and she chalks it up as one more good reason to love this man.

Jeff slides into the booth beside her, plants a quick one on her left cheek and asks,

"How's my bride, today?" Calliope returns, "I'm good baby, how are you?"

"I'm good now, my beautiful. Your face is my therapy. How did your session, go?"

"It was good. He seems nice." Calliope offers little else. There is no need.

Jeff gives back a "Hmmm." And a furrowed brow. Nothing more.

What does that look mean? She starts to ask him but then she tucks it away because she remembers watching an interview with Diane Sawyer wherein Diane said:

"So what if he leaves a banana peel on the counter- this is a GOOD man."

Since The Incident, Calliope never sweats the small stuff and the category for small stuff grows larger each day.

A waitress appears and greets what she determines to be Barbie and Ken. She may or may not have recognized Cee Cee. Calliope senses the competitive nature in her and tries to be extra sweet when ordering.

It's silly how girls feel like we compete with every bat of an eye.

She does not win her over, instead causing the waitress to begin a tiny flirtation with her husband.

"What are we having, handsome?" the flirty hussy beckons.

Yeah, honey as if "we" includes "you".

Now Cee Cee knows this girl does indeed recognize her and just cannot help herself.

Calliope intentionally ignores this attempt because this is not the first time a girl tried to pry Jeff away and because Calliope deeply feels that if anyone could get him, they could have him. She is his and only his. He needs to be hers as well. That's only fair.

Calliope orders the Hawaiian Hump because it is her favorite entrée. It disgusts her that the owner feels the need to use sexual innuendo in naming his selections. The burger sells itself with a thick slice of Canadian bacon and a wedge of fresh, grilled pineapple. It does not need a dirty name. Jeff has his usual Patty's Big, Big Boy and consumes it quickly.

"I was famished," Calliope says as she pops in the last bite of Hump.

 "Me, too," Jeff returns, "I skipped lunch today."

"Don't you just love the word famished? It's like it just crawls up out of you. Famished…"

Jeff answers, "I do indeed. And I love you because you think about it that way."

Calliope lets out a feminine little explosion and remarks, "That was even a delicious burp." Jeff laughs.

Calliope knows she will taste it again later when she forces the popsicle stick down her throat.

All Your Ducks in a Row

PJ is writing in her diary. Writing and thinking about coal miners. She has just watched a documentary on *The History Channel* about the men who earn their living deep in the earth, beneath tectonic plates. She is astounded to discover that miners willingly load themselves like sheep into tiny metal carts and descend deep into the earth, into an unstable shelter that collapses, coats their lungs and makes it difficult to take in breath. She can relate. Her obsession is eating her from the inside out and she likens it to a mountain opening up to swallow its native sons. Her thoughts are interrupted by Brad.

"Hey, honeybun. What's for lunch?" PJ is startled and quickly closes her diary.

"Hi, baby. I did not know you would be home. What would you like? I have some leftover pork loin from last night and macaroni and cheese. I think there is still some of that creamed corn that I scraped off the cob. Or, I could just make you a Greek pizza."

"I don't want you to trouble yourself, sweetness, but Greek pizza sounds fabulous." Brad answers her.

"OK, boo bear. You got it," she reciprocates.

PJ stands and taking her diary with her, she walks to the restroom. She stashes her written thoughts underneath the cabinet with the sink, just behind the tampons and hygiene cloths.

He will NEVER look there.

Truth be known, he doesn't even pay enough attention to see that she is writing anything nor does he know she even owns a diary. A man tunes in for about five minutes and out at the mention of food.

PJ flushes the toilet for good measure and a cover story, washes her hands thoroughly and walks to the kitchen.

She opens the stainless doors of her refrigerator and removes a bag of pre-washed spinach, a small jar of pesto, a gallon jug of Kalamata olives and a small block of feta cheese. She pre-heats the matching stainless oven to 375 degrees and retrieves a baking pan from the cabinet to her lower left beside the kitchen sink. She lays the pan on the stovetop and bends down again to grab a cutting board. Walking toward the silver ware caddy, she selects a Rada tomato knife and returns to the stove. The tallest cabinet houses extra virgin olive oil. PJ retrieves it, grabs a small paint brush from the nearest drawer and paints a coating on the pan. Then she searches the lower food cabinet for pita bread and not finding any, she grabs the gordita shells and opens them. PJ pulls four breads from the package, then re-seals it at the top. She places the flour pancakes on the baking pan.

PJ opens the pesto jar and with a small spoon that is lying on the counter, then pastes a thin layer on each gordita shell. The spinach is still where she left it so she opens it and arranges 6-8 leaves on each potential pizza. PJ loves creating her food and fancies it to flower arranging. She especially loves the marriage of color. The deep green of the spinach accented by the vivid red of the Romas and the stark white splashes of feta. Sometimes in her head, she imagines herself on her own cooking show: *Pastries of PJ* or *Mediterranean Mama* even though she does not have the knowledge or skill to pull something like that off. It is still fun to play dress up!

PJ unwraps a large brick of feta, rich and uneven, it reminds her of a creamy styrofoam cooler. She breaks off generous boulders of the salty block and sets it aside.

Peyton uses the cutting board to slice the olives and the Roma tomatoes. She always carefully removes all the seeds from the tomato which gives it a red pepper resemblance. She does this in memory of her grandfather and his battle with diverticulosis. And she does it out of habit as well. PJ is adding the final touches and placing the pan into the oven when she hears the quacking.

From the other room, Brad hollers, "Hey! Your duck is back."

Peyton enters the living room, picks up her cell phone from the coffee table, powers it on, slides the screen right and says: "Hello?"

"Mrs. Anderson?" the caller inquires.

"Yes, this is she," Peyton answers her.

"This is Miss Honeycut, Dr. Fisher's executive secretary. We have an opening for you next week. Are you available for 3:30 pm on Thursday?"

"Yes, thank you. I will make that happen." PJ quickly closes up her phone and powers it off.

"Who that be?" Brad asks.

"Cheryl from the Rotary Club. They want me to head up a project. She needs me start next week." PJ is lying of course.

"Using and abusing. You have to learn to say no, Peege."

You have no idea how right you are.

Sessions

Vinnie Gives It Up

Vinnie exits the cab he hailed four streets ago and enters the medical high rise. He rides to the fourth floor and enters Dr. Fisher's office. He doesn't greet Miss Honeycut as they are way past pleasantries and she was never pleasant in the first place so he feels no obligation to cough up cordial. She knows why he is here. He does not need to announce it.

"Dr. Fisher will see you now."

She gets whinier each time if that is possible!

Vinnie enters the doctor's lair and chooses the high cushion once again.

After brief superficial exchanges, Dr. Fisher states: "Today, Mr. Castana, I would like to begin my hypnotherapy with you. Are you in agreement with that?"

"Youse the doc, but I have to ax a couple questions before we go."

"OK, what are your concerns?" Fisher responds.

"Well, I needs to know if youse can read my memory when youse has me in that condition?" Vinnie baits him with the question.

"Whatever do you mean?" Fisher replies.

"Youse know, like can you see things I've done that I maybe, youse know, wants to keep to myself," Vinnie stammers.

"Mr. Castana, you will be dictating how the session goes. You will have more control over how and what is done than I will. I will simply suggest things to your psyche that you and I have agreed to in advance."

"Whoa, whoa there doc. Youse never said nothing about no psyches. I am Catholic. We don't do psyches. That is witchcraft," Vinnie delivers.

And then a voice, like conscience, whispers……

"I will cut off witchcrafts out of thine hand; and thou shalt have no more soothsayers." Micah 5:12

"Psyche, Mr. Castana." There is no readable expression on the doctor's face.

Really, I have to explain this?

"Not psychic. Psyche refers only to the state of your mind," Steven explains.

"That is why you has the degree with letters on it," Vinnie answers not at all embarrassed about his Archie Bunker ignorance.

 "Doc, you won't be signing any scrips for me, will youse?"

"Mr. Castana, what are you currently taking? Did you need a refill?" Steven asks him.

"No, I was just axing you because my family doctor took me off my meds-they made me too aggressive," Vinnie informs him.

Steven muffles a laugh, then chokes and passes it off as a cough.

"Very well. Now that we have settled that, I will begin by explaining exactly how hypnotherapy works," Steven instructs.

"Fire away, doc." And then Vinnie the Weasel laughs heartily. He will not share his private joke with his physician but the fire away comment makes him think on the good doctor's future………

Sessions

Peyton

Dr. Fisher sits with his mouth wide open. "I am sorry. You want me to do what?!"

Steven is arrogant enough to think that no one patient can throw him, but this woman has done just that.

"I want you to tell my brain to forget about someone. I am in misery, doctor. I cannot stop thinking about him. I can't stay off Facebook hoping he will hop on at any moment. I have never been this way about social media. I scroll faces, not Facebook. This man is consuming me from the inside out. I don't have what it takes to control it and so I want you to control those thoughts in me."

Steven, still dumbfounded, sits without speaking for a bit.

When he does speak, it is slowly and with reservation. "Well, I have certainly never been asked to do that before."

Peyton Jane begins to weep. As she is sobbing, she asks him,

"Well, is it even a possibility? I can't go on like this-I need to get over it now!"

Just then PJ is enveloped in instantaneous grief, the kind that takes you over and tears begin streaming down your cheeks before you even feel the real emotion of it. A grief that gravitates South before your mind or heart can begin to process what has just happened. The same one you experience when you get that phone call informing you a parent is gone. Before you have time to fully feel it, your sinuses have put on two pounds in ten seconds snuffing up sick sniffles through the burning nostrils of faux cocaine grief.

Peyton wimpers: "And I am so damn mad at him."

Steven looks confused. "Who, the Facebook man?"

"Yes, him. Him indeed. If I am the subject of that email, if he did hold all this affection for me 30 years ago, then why reveal it now? What am I supposed to do with that information, anyway? Break a good man's heart? Question my life and the value of it? Drop everything for him? Facebook has made him brave, given him cyber courage. How dare he! How dare he make me wonder…what if? I am a good Christian woman."

Now I hate you.

 Steven hates religion on any level.

"This isn't how I act. This isn't how I feel." Peyton attempts to explain.

"It is definitely a painful conundrum for you. I have never done what you are asking me to do, but I am not telling you that I won't try just yet. I do, however, need to consult with a colleague, (*big, fat, hairy lie*), before moving ahead or making any decision about your treatment. I hope that is an acceptable arrangement for you," Dr. Fisher returns.

"Very well. Thank you for your time today. I hope to hear from you soon," Peyton finishes up as she slides away snot which is still freely flowing down her face.

PJ rises and swipes away the wrinkles that have formed in her cotton pants adjusting her outfit so as to be presentable to the outside of his office. She starts for the door and then turning, faces Dr. Fisher and ends with:

"Doctor."

"Yes," he answers.

"You won't use my name when you discuss me with your colleague, will you?"

Steven reassures her, "Absolutely not. Your secret is safe with me."

Vinnie's Second Exodus

Vinnie leaves the medical complex, hails another cab and marks out for home. From the backseat, he checks the rear view mirror. He checks it again. And again. He will check it six more times before arriving, force of habit. He is always watching, always waiting for his number to be called.

Vinnie stays on his toes because he knows he can never be a made man. It is a genetic trick that prevents his advancement, a chance meeting on a train. His mother, Anjelique and his father, Anthony, finding each other and so in love do not concern themselves with the thought that their offspring will not benefit from that one quarter French messing with his Sicilian stamp of approval. Vinnie is as good as a half-breed and as high on the mob roster as he will ever go. Might as well go ahead and draw a target on his back. Eventually, he will be a liability.

The cab slows in front of Vinnie's east side residence in the area of Harlem known as Little Italy. Vinnie resides in a dilapidated apartment building on 116th. Street, just east of Madison Avenue.

He unlocks the outside door with a skeleton key and walks the two flights up to his matchbox apartment. As he enters, he breathes in the simmering Italian orgasm that is his dinner. Analisa, his love and wife, is setting the table and presenting his meal as she has every evening for 37 years. Vinnie takes his place at the head of a two-seater. Analisa's barren womb has presented no need to increase the table size.

Vinnie gazes at this woman as she spoons noodles to his plate with two large utensils. The spittle flows freely down both sides of his throat as she dresses it with sauce and peppers it with fresh Parmigiano. Vinnie stretches for a stiff piece of bread, baptizes it in red sauce and lifts it to his mouth.

"Mama Mia! Youse outdone youself!" Vinnie is almost singing his delight.

Analisa sputters back, "Eh, you-a say that-a every time-a!"

"And every time it is true!" Vinnie uses his spoon to knit his noodles into a small ball and drops it into his mouth. With every bite, he thinks: *I love this woman. I love this woman. I LOVE THIS WOMAN.*

"You want-a some more?" Analisa asks him. "Si, amor," he flirts back.

"Don' you-a go and try-a seduce me. I got-a dishes to do," Analisa flirts in retaliation. Analisa leans into the sauce bowl scooping a heaping helping to his plate, her panic alert button clacking against cherry veneer. Vinnie insists on the panic button not just for her health but in case she has a visit from his mob friends. He cares for her, so he takes care of her. Vinnie's mother, the revered, (*cue holy music*) had recently died alone in the duplex Vinnie provided for her, undiscovered for a week.

  The flies, Vinnie remembers. The scavengers had eaten at her face leaving the image of congenital syphilis, pre-penicillin.

Madre. *His* mind could not, would not, shake the image.

A housefly lands on the edge of the porcelain pasta bowl, pausing and flicking its wings.

Aye, Madre.

Roll-A-Drama

PJ is feeling nostalgic.

It is probably all this petty girl crush stuff transporting me back to high school where I would watch Cyrano from afar. I cannot seem to stop listening to the oldies station as if my potential adultery needs some sort of theme song. It is distressing to think my music is classified as the oldies now and here I sit contemplating destroying everything I love for some tawdry afternoon romp with a man who looks older than my father. Oh God! Is that it? Is that the attraction?

Am I just drumming up ghosts from a patriarch long planted? I have never stopped seeking the elusive, mystery man who ran out on my mother when I had just begun to toddle. Will Brad cut me some slack if he finds out and I use that as my excuse?

Don't fool yourself, woman. That little girl is as dead as your daddy. You may be driving yourself to a roller rink, but you can't turn the timepiece back and you can't resurrect demons almost thirty years old.

Peyton continues on her drive to Whirl-A-Rama justifying her jump back to junior high as much needed exercise. When she arrives, she removes her scarred and dusty skates from the back of her SUV and enters through the front door of the roller rink. She is surprised to discover that roller rinks are not the hit they once were and that she is pretty much going to be skating by herself except for the preschool children who are here accompanied by their teacher. And there are only nine of those.

Peyton sits on a weathered bench and removes her Keds. She slips her feet carefully into her antiquated roller skates and attempts to rise. Amazingly she does not immediately fall and manages to recall some of the moves she used to make on skates. She circles the rink for about an hour, enjoying the slight breeze disturbing her hair and even attempting some fancier foot moves alongside one attempt to skate backwards.

The repeated rings she makes around the floor are therapeutic. Peyton is thinking deep, pathetic thoughts today. Dark ideas welling from inside about her character, her voice and her innate ability to read people. She is desperately trying to read herself.

Cyrano was so quiet in school. I am anything but still. Perhaps those who run quieter, stilling the noise inside, never picking fights with themselves stand a bit closer to the edge. Maybe they are poised to leap.

If we are what we think, am I just all that nails me to my past? I am Rock Em Sock Em Robots, Necco Wafers, The Monkees and bell bottom blue jeans. And I am a roller rink. I feel more like a pair of Clackers, most of which are still wound around the telephone lines we slung them onto years ago, perilously pitching toward the ground.

Peyton concludes she has done all the skating her knees and hips can stand and decides to head for the restroom before she removes her skates. She fails to recall that inside floors are much icier than outside floors and that the bathroom floor in a roller rink is akin to dried, pressed Crisco.

Peyton needs to pee. So she sails into the restroom struggling to maintain her balance and an upright position. She pulls herself hand over hand into an open stall. Once she is safely seated, it comes to her attention that the stall door is malfunctioning and refusing to fasten itself, so she pulls it to with one hand. Besides, the process of getting here and seating herself is far too involved to turn back now and attempt another placement. Peyton pees. As she tries to return to her standing position, she begins to roll. Peyton is frozen in a squatted position too frightened to go up and unable to go back down. The broken door gives way and she continues in her squatted position, with her jeans around her ankles, one arm extended for balance and the other arm wildly waving a piece of unused toilet paper.

On she rolls, her squashed, dripping, naked roll until she strikes the adjacent wall. After the collision, PJ crawls the parapet by hand, reassembles her clothing and what is left of her pride.

Well, this pretty much sums up my life right now. One humiliation after another.

Sessions – Vinnie

Head Games

Steven continues questioning Vinnie and Vinnie does not like this line of questioning.

"Now, Mr. Castana, back to your family medical history for a moment. Are you aware of any instances of mental illness or psychotic episodes that have occurred in any family member in close proximity to you?" Steven is nothing if not thorough.

Vinnie snaps back and his face is spewing venom, "Don't youse talk about my family, Doc!"

"Mr. Castana, I assure you, it is a necessary part of your treatment to establish a medical history. It is the only way I can insure a safe course of treatment for you. I am going into your mind, and I need to know if there is a predilection for any permanent damage before I do so."

Vinnie still on the defensive and precarious, comes back with,

"Why? What have youse heard?"

"Once again, Mr. Castana, I assure you I have no preconceived notions about you or any of your relatives. I am simply establishing a base line for your treatment." Steven is exhausted.

It is like training a toddler.

Vinnie looks confused.

OK, Steven dumb it down.

"It could result in permanent damage to you. A permanent impairment." The doctor is trying to explain it.

More confusion for Vinnie.

"It might mess up your head!" Steven, exasperated, is almost screaming.

"Oh, ok Doc. I got youse. I do have one cousin who ain't never been right. She took scarlet fever when she was a baby and it never left her head."

 Vinnie's generosity about his family history is completely out of character.

"That is more environmental…." Steven notices the confused look on Vinnie's face. He spares him the humiliation of a vocabulary lesson.

 "That won't hurt you. You should be fine," the doctor assures Vinnie.

"That is a relief, Doc. I am a little understuffed upstairs."

That is the understatement of the year.

First Do No Harm

Sessions: Calliope Tape Two

The voice on the tape is Steven's and then it is
Calliope's.

This is Dr. Steven Fisher, MD

My patient, Calliope Cash, is seated on my office
couch and the following is an auditory transcript of our
session today.

"I have got to figure this out. I just signed a huge deal
with Hypothesis Jeans and I must be in control. I
overeat, even when I am not the least bit hungry."
Steven watches a clear path of seepage racing down
Calliope's face. He offers her a tissue. There is a
rustling sound picked up on the audio as she rises to
receive it.

"It's ….it's…so…..I am monumentally ashamed of this
and I am also embarrassed because I actually look
forward to the moment when I can release my last
meal into a sink or toilet. I even use a thermos which
I intentionally bring from home," Calliope is weeping
persistent water.

Steven uses a calm inflection and lies to comfort his
patient.

"Miss Cash, I have had great success treating bulimia
with hypnotherapy. Even the most addictive
personalities have been known to respond in just a
few sessions, usually seven or less. With your

permission, I would like to administer a little questionnaire to see how likely you are to respond."

"Doctor, I do not have a choice in the matter. I absolutely have to fix this and I do not have much time. My Hypothesis campaign takes off in six and a half months," Calliope answers him.

"Well, then clearly every moment is critical so let us begin," Steven goes on.

"Ok, I'm game." Calliope wipes away incessant snot. More rustling is heard on the audio.

"Calliope, do you like to read books, novels and such?" Dr. Fisher queries.

"Sure," she responds.

"Calliope, when you read, do you find yourself getting caught up in the story?" Steven baits her.

"If it is a good book, I do indeed. Jeff, um, my friend Jeff, complains that I don't have ears when I am reading!" Calliope says correcting her slip.

Steven looks at a clipboard, jots down a note and then continues,

 "Would you say that you get certain songs stuck in your head replaying over and over?"

"Yeah, but I thought everyone did that!" Steven makes a notation.

"Are you prone to daydreaming?" Steven inquires.

"Mmm hmm." Another notation.

"Will an emotional movie cause you to cry or express a parallel sentiment?" Steven continues on.

"I could confidently reply almost always, but again it has to be a good movie just like the book. And they cannot change the ending. I hate it when they do that," Calliope responds.

Again Steven makes a small notation and then announces:

"Miss Cash, I am pleased to inform you it appears you would likely be an excellent candidate for this type of therapy and I am excited to see where this will go."

Dr.Fisher is pleased with himself and the results of his poll.

"Oh, Dr. Fisher, I am so happy to hear that," Calliope exclaims.

If only you knew my plans for you, my pretty.

Vinnie Makes Good

Vincent Castana strolls the city streets like he owns them. If fear is any indicator of ownership, then he isn't that far from right. Vinnie is feeling relieved this day as he exits Sparks Steakhouse after his meeting with Boss. As he passes over the pavement where Godfather Paul Castellano was assassinated, he genuflects and signs the cross out of respect. He considers this hallowed ground. A great man met his maker here.

Vinnie continues walking east on 46th. He is scanning for a street vendor that pitches peanuts and coconut. Analisa loves the toasted coconut and he intends to find her some. Vinnie is traveling behind an obese woman with the arms of a sumo wrestler. She is "wearing" an undersized tank top and the straps are heading South at an alarming rate. It frightens him to think what he is about to witness. Her capri yoga pants are yellow and he can make out the distinct outline of her G-string underwear. Smiling to himself, he thinks:

Youse can snag a whale on a two-pound test.

Analisa is a lady and she always dresses the part. So Vinnie is unforgiving when it comes to women and their decency. Quickly he hastens his pace in order to change the scenery.

Two blocks from the restaurant, Vincent can smell the vendor before he actually sees him. The sign on his cart reads:

Peanuts, Cashews, Pecans and Coconut-three bundles for nine dollars.

Vinnie saunters to the cart and places his order for two coconuts and one pecan. The vendor opens the first metal door and reaches in deep to scoop out a cup of sugared pecans. He places them in the paper cone and then reaches in again. After filling the first cone, he taps down on the sides and seals it like a gift. He repeats the same process twice in the coconut bin and pushes three packages toward Vinnie. He does not ask for the nine dollars. Vinnie knows he won't. Vainly, Vinnie reaches into his left pants pocket and pulls out a thick rolled up wad of bills in all denominations from hundreds to ones with the hundreds on the outside in plain view. He works the wad with his dampened thumb for a minute or two seeming to consider payment or a tip and then rerolls it and returns it to his left front pocket. He reaches for his coconut and pecans.

"Thank youse and youse have a good day," is the only payment Vinnie offers the man. Vinnie likes this game. It is Godfatherish.

"Yessir and you as well," is the vendor's only answer.

Vinnie continues walking toward East 47th Street and the Church of the Holy Trinity. Father Francesco is the residing priest and Vinnie has scheduled a confession with him. Vinnie keeps the good Father busy but he has not yet blown out about that business with Tommy. The Weasel approaches the cement building which always reminds him of a pyramid instead of a church and enters through the Rectory door. Father Francesco is speaking with a parishioner in the corridor but nods when he sees Vinnie and quickly ends his conversation.

Smiling and extending his arms, he embraces the repentant hit man.

"Vincent. It has been-a too long I no see you. You make-a me so happy this-a day."

"Frankie. How youse doin?" Vinnie returns.

"Good, my brother. Very good. Have you-a seen our sister recently?" the good father asks.

"Not since mama passed. But I will go to her as soon as youse absolve me, brother."

"Yes, this-a way." Father Francesco tells him.

It is extremely convenient for Vinnie that one of his five siblings is a priest. It keeps the secrets in the family. Italian families are tighter than a wasp's nest. While Father Frankie does not approve of Vinnie's occupation, as his brother and priest, it is still his place to absolve him of it. With this, he holds no issue. And Vinnie has no reason to sustain any guilt over his activities because he receives almost instantaneous absolution. But without a conscience, he simply goes through the motions of repentance and considers it icing on the cake. Confession is merely his Catholic requirement.

"Forgive me Father, for I have sinned. It has been ten days since my last confession."

"Continue my son," Father Frank responds.

"I coveted a woman I saw on the street. I spoke in anger to a friend who didn't deserve it. And I whacked Tommy the Mick O'Toole."

Father Frank has seen this seat many times before this confession. He knows better than to advise Vinnie to go to the police and confess his crime and besides, this is his brother. His blood. *His veins, my veins*. Even a priest won't rat out his blood. So instead of scolding him he says,

"Do you-a repent of these sins and wish-a to be absolved?"

"Absolutely," Vinnie barks back.

"Then-a do twelve Hail Marys and light-a three candles. One-a for each-a infraction. And go-a in-a peace my son."

The way Vinnie sees it, that is that. He has fulfilled his duty and there is no reason to think on it ever again.

Vincent exits the Rectory and walks to the curb to hail a cab. Within just a minute a yellow taxi slows and Vinnie enters the vehicle. The driver, born and bred Queens, asks,

"Where you wanna be?"

Vinnie responds,

"Hundred and thirty-fifth street. Near the mahket."

The driver knows exactly where he is taking his charge from the brief description. He starts his meter and drives East to one hundred and thirty-fifth. Upon arrival, he gives Vinnie his total, $29.75, and then bites his bottom lip to see if Vinnie will actually make good this time. Vinnie reaches into his left pants pocket for the second time and casually peels back ones, fives, tens, twenties and stops at fifties. He slides one fresh, crisp fifty-dollar bill from the obnoxious wad and gives it to the cabbie. Although out of character for Vincent, his fresh, clean soul leaves him feeling generous.

Sessions

Calliope Number Nine

"Your eyes are so, so heavy, little girl," Steven instructs.

"Are they?" Calliope asks opening them.

"Yes," he plants. "And you need to close them." Calliope does as she is told. Her lids slowly pull back together.

She is becoming my girl.

And Steven feels less culpability when she does not witness his orchestrations of her.

"Now, little girl, imagine that you are at Fab Patty's. You have just finished your favorite meal."

Calliope begins to lick her lips lightly and say, "Mmm it's so good." Calliope's "mmm" stirs in Steven's slacks.

"I know it is. Eat it all. It tastes so delicious," Steven leads her.

"It does, it really does. I almost hate to throw it back up," Calliope surrenders.

"You don't have to this time. This time, the meal will stay where you left it," he plants.

"Ok. I need to go to the ladies' room, I think," Calliope responds.

"Not this time. Not this time at all," Steven plants. "You are still hungry little girl," Steven coaxes her.

"Yes, I am," she obediently responds.

"Order dessert," he continues.

"I will, daddy," she replies. Steven loves it when she calls him daddy. He should love it, HE planted it there.

"So, do you have any cheesecake, no wait, I want cannoli," she requests from an imaginary waitress.

"That's my girl," he teases her.

"It looks delicious. Can I have it now? Daddy, may I?" Steven can barely contain himself.

"Yes, you may. Here it is."

Then Calliope's face disappears in Steven's lap.

PJ's Diary

Dear Stupid Pages,

I am miserable. I have no idea what I am doing and I also know exactly what I am doing. And I cannot stop. I am being eaten just like <u>Attack of the Killer Tomatoes</u>- consumed by a goopy red heart.

I cannot sleep. It is 3:04 am. It is not insomnia so much but rather one nagging sentence I need to put to paper. The one that won't be still so I can sleep. The same one that causes me to rise, wipe the night from my face, and turn 16 words into 2000.

Truthfully, it's that sentence and a hot flash. How dare that little splash of physiology wake me? The ghostly unnamed fire igniting at the soles of my feet and continuing its creep up my core until it reaches my face and explodes from every pore. And I sweat. A tiny bursting flame releasing my final bits of girl. And how dare a menopausal middle-aged-woman whose flesh does not even respond any more think about having an affair? What enjoyment will I even get from it? Nothing feels the same as if parts of me, the good ones I have left, are simply expired. Overstayed their welcome, out of here. I used to get aroused when Brad just looked hard at me or with those "right now" eyes and now, nuttin' honey. We love each other desperately it is just that our bodies don't remember. Is this why the prospect of Cyrano is so inviting? That perhaps he, and only he, can stir something buried deep within me? Or maybe dig out that one thing that never is fully satisfied?

I never used to understand women who were willing to risk it all for an afternoon. I thought them tawdry and undisciplined. Yet even as sweat beads line up against my night dress resisting the cohosh taken earlier, I tremble at the thought of resurrecting or insurrecting sensations I have long put away.

I imagine us. I cannot shake the image in my mind of his lips barely brushing mine, teasing me intelligently. Blowing and wettening my nipples until my groin is begging for him to enter. Old flesh brought to life and then he, inside, searching my expression with those soulful, grey, magnificent eyes. He knows me and I am powerless to resist him. I think he might be the devil. And that kind of makes me want it even more. It's like forbidden fruit exemplified.

I can even picture us washing off the day and my shame and the passion and his liquid. And then his hands forming around my waist from behind and it is feral. It is amazing. And it is only in my mind.

And now diary as I reread this, I remember and imagine someone else. Me. Last year me. The dutiful wife and the only one at the Rotary Club who still loves and has no bad review of her spouse. The other women harbor a little resentment over that. If they only knew now what I am thinking, they'd all grab a caramel macchiato and have a session about it. That conversation would be a doozy. Things like:

"Can you get her nerve? And always playing like all is perfect..."

"Oh, she didn't fool me, I always knew she was capable of that."

"I just feel so sorry for the children having a whore mother and all."

"Poor Brad, I wonder if he needs some consoling..." followed by random giggles and the raising of hands. My Brad is a looker if I have to say so myself.

So where did that PJ go? I am still so stinking confused about how I can be content with one man one day and consumed by another the next. I have been to Africa, a third world country for Pete's sake. That technically makes me a missionary and I am on the edge of breaking a pretty big commandment.

And about that mission trip-I'd like to say it changed me, skewed my perspective. That it reached deep down and dug out my compassion making me a kinder, gentler, a better version of myself. Of who I thought I was anyway. I hoped it would alter my reality but it did not. I witnessed unparalleled poverty in a country with no church resources, no city missions no YMCA housing units and as I sit here there are thirty-nine handbags in my closet and an undisclosed number of pairs of shoes. The rod housing my wardrobe actually collapsed once from the weight and the number of garments and had to be replaced with a steel bar. I live a life of frivolity while indigent families farm a ground that betrays them. Shame on me. Shame on me for all of it.

Vinnie the Robot

Vinnie gravitates more than walks down the sidewalk on his way home that evening. He simply cannot remember where he has been or why. Absolutely no details of his day. None whatsoever. It is the weirdest experience to know that you should know what just happened and to be completely aware that you are clueless. It's as if he has lost time.

This must be what amnesia feels like.

 And then he vaguely remembers hearing his mother talk about feeling this way when she hemorrhaged after giving birth to him. In his mind he sees a conversation of which he could have no possible memory.

Words from The Revered:

 "The doctor, he-a say, Mrs. Castana, what type of birth control do you use? I look-a up at Carmine and say, what is-a birth control? The doctor he no laugh even though he probably think-a of course she don't know, she just have-a baby. If she did-a know, she no have-a baby. I know I should-a know, but I can't think-a clearly at that time. They say later it was-a because I had-a no iron left in my blood. From-a the bleeding."

"That's how it feels, Mama. I feels like I cannot remember things, I gots no recollection. And Mama, I'm not sure if I'm not remembering or just gettings old. Or maybe just losing my mind. I need youse here with me. I miss youse every day."

 Vinnie still communicates with his matriarch regularly because he is convinced she hears every single utterance. He still watches his mouth, too. Vinnie doesn't fancy getting slapped by a Catholic specter.

Vinnie slides the key into the lock on his apartment door and Analisa greets him at the door.

"Whatsa matter you? I cook-a all day and you show-a up at this hour? Only the rounders is-a out at this-a hour! What you thinking?"

Vinnie does not smile. He does not kiss his wife. He does not even smell the remnant of his dinner simmering on low. He still has the coconuts in his outer coat pocket, but he has no recollection of purchasing them so they stay where they are. His eyes hold a look of death, zombie-ish. Of being there, and not being there. It's all in the eyes.

"Do you hear me-a talking with you? Do you?" Analisa sounds desperate now.

Analisa rarely raises her voice beyond typical Italian wife, but right now old Vinnie is ticking her off. Unless he is having a massive stroke, he is about to get it.

"Vincent Carmine Castana! Do you hear me?" Analisa screams.

And at the sound of his full name, indeed he does.

PJ Thinks It Through

*A million sins are rolling around in my head.
Tomorrow is the first session and all I have done
today is Google hypnosis and related topics. I have
to remember to ask Dr. Fisher about hetero-hypnosis.
The online article states it is usually implemented to
conquer a defeatist attitude so maybe he can use that
technique to help me defeat myself and my out of
control obsession for Cyrano. I wish I could stop. I
just can't. My head is too screwed up to think clearly
and even today as I googled hypnosis, I kept
checking my messenger app and scrolling for his
comments on Facebook and Twitter.*

*That article said that the National Football League
uses hypnosis to help the players ignore the pain.
That just might work. I hope I do not ignore the pain.
I want to stay completely aware of the hurt I will cause
Brad if he ever finds out about this. I have got to nip
this in the bud. Erase it. Get over my middle-aged
ego and the romantic idea of someone new.
Someone different. There is nothing wrong with my
husband, he is damn near perfect. So what is wrong
with me?*

PJ slides in her slippers toward the kitchen and
rearranges the donut pieces still lying on a plate on
the counter. She cuts each pastry into four sections,
just like her mother used to do, and organizes them
according to their current level of deliciousness:
chocolate, filled and plain glazed. She selects the last
raspberry filled quarter, squeezes the bloody contents
into her mouth and wipes the powdered sugar coating
blanketing her upper lip onto the back of her hand.

Well, it certainly won't help anything if I can't get into my jeans tomorrow. As if contemplating adultery isn't self-loathing enough, I have to top it off with deep fried lard. Delicious, deep fried lard.

I hate the devil. I know enough about the Bible to know he is behind all of this. Call yourself a Christian and you might as well paint a target on your back. And get ready for the attack because it is coming.

He is so stinking sneaky. He knows exactly how to package this man to make him irresistible to me. Make him a wordsmith. Have him write me a poem. Give him deep thoughts and he is as lethal to my resolve as Brad Pitt was to Angelina.

And a voice like conscience whispers....

Thou shalt not commit adultery. Exodus 20:14

I know! I know! I am working on it.

Waking Up

It's three minutes before the alarm is set to sound and Jeff rolls to the left side of the bed, spooning with his bride. She stirs and wakes slightly.

He whispers into her ear, "I got my hot dog in your bun and my arm under your boobie."

"Then you missed," his sleepy bride responds. Laughter erupts from the left side of the bed in unison with the whine of 430 am.

"That stupid thing is broken," Cee Cee whispers to her husband.

"The clock?" Jeff asks.

 Calliope yawns an answer. "Yes, the clock. It goes off earlier every day."

"Ha, ha. Get up buttercup, you almost had me there," Jeff teases. "You have a big day, girlfriend."

"Oh, I know. A set shoot. I hate those, they always want you to do something stupid like dive underwater or they paint you like a peacock and tell you to give them sexy. Someone in the universe please explain how a sexy peacock actually looks!" Calliope banters on.

"Did they tell you anything about it?" Jeff presses.

"Nope. Just that they constructed a special set to kick off the campaign and asked me if I was afraid of heights," Calliope gives back.

"Did you lie to them?" Jeff asks.

"Well, yeah, of course I did. I AM under contract. I cannot very well tell them I am terrified of heights after I signed on the dotted line and they constructed a three hundred-thousand-dollar tower or whatever it is, can I?" Calliope sasses.

"I guess not. Educated guess that is. Hypothesis, really. Ha, ha. No pun intended." Jeff snickers, amusing only himself.

"Yea, you're a funny guy, husband of mine." Calliope tries to appear unamused but Jeff recognizes that tiny smile as her image passes the mirror hanging over the oak dresser. He knows that smile well. And he thinks:

I love this woman. I love this woman. I LOVE THIS WOMAN.

Vinnie's in the House

Vinnie's nose catches the scent of the simmer.
"Analisa, mi amore, is that Bolognese?"

"Vincent Carmine Castana!" He is fully aware now.
And monumentally confused.

"Analisa! Why is youse screaming at me?"

"Vincent, tell-a me what-a just happen to you-a! You-a
havin' a stroke or what? Tell-a me the truth, husband!"
Analisa has the desperate look of a tired zebra being
chased by a lion with no escape route. "Tell-a me,
now!"

"What youse mean?" Vinnie questions, clueless that
he is Steven's pawn in a sinister game of chess. He
has no idea what level of control he has handed to
this man. And he holds no answer to her question.

Analisa embellishes, "You-a no-a answer me when I
ask-a you-a something. Your face it-a freeze and you-
a look-a far away. Like you-a no-a here with me."

"What is youse talking about, Analisa?" Vinnie still
held her name in his mouth as if he were sampling
Beluga caviar, still so enamored of his bride.

 "I answer youse now."

"NOT NOW, Vincent! Before when I-a ask you-a, you-
a act-a like a statue of the Good Mother," Analisa
explains.

Now the wheels in Vinnie's head begin to turn. He
has never lost time before and in his profession, this
is a precarious place to rest. Vinnie, above all others,

needs to know exactly where he has been, what he has said and how he has acted. Because every tiny thing must to be reported back to Boss.

And even though a brief conversation with Vinnie would make you believe he ain't the sharpest knife in the drawer, Vinnie is not stupid. He has street smarts, he knows the code and his common sense rating is off the chart. So he is starting to put it all together. He is seeing a hypnotherapist-the physician's main skill not lost on Vinnie.

If that fugazi has done something, they will never locate all the pieces......

Analisa is still shaken by her husband's robotic lapse. Offset, she inquires,

"Where you-a go today?"

"I seen Boss at Sparks, I went to confession with Frankie, and then I seen Carmella," Vinnie lists as he strains to recall his day. The memories of his activities are slowly returning and becoming clearer in his head.

"Ah, Carmella. I no see-a her in ages. How-a she doin'?" Analisa switches topics quickly.

"Not so good, amor. The cancer eats a little each day. She is weak." Vinnie is both sad and defeated.

"Dios mio, I go-a to her tomorrow," Analisa laments. "What-a else, Vincent?"

Vincent slips his hands into his pants pocket, a habit with no purpose and locates the cones. He is shocked to find them but disguises his surprise. His wife is already upset, no reason to make her think her husband may have Alzheimer's as well.

"I stop to get youse some coconuts." His chubby, scarred hands capture the cones and bring them to the surface. The pecans met a swifter demise.

"Vincent, you-a know me so well. Ok,ok, I forget all the rest." Analisa finally surrenders.

Vincent opts not tell his wife he has no idea how those coconuts ended up in his pockets. He also has no recollection of his appointment with Dr. Fisher just after he left the street vendor. He can vaguely recall parts of the day but just like an alcoholic blackout, some of the pieces are missing.

He watches intently as Analisa heads for the kitchen, turns and smiles coyly at him biting the top of her wooden spoon.

Calliope on Set

The French director, Bernard Baxter, is the indisputable boss. He runs the show no matter who the real person in charge is supposed to be. He believes every word of his own PR, the good, the bad and the ugly. His name isn't even real, a Hollywood concoction. It's always an alliteration: Marilyn Monroe, Calliope Cash, Bernard Baxter.

This commercial shoot, even though it is attached to a solid industry brand, is truly beneath him. A criminal accountant has crippled his selectivity and he is resentful about even being on this particular set.

And because Bernard's time truly is more important than anyone else's, he does not tolerate a diva. He suggested Calliope for the Hypothesis campaign because he knows her to be punctual and professional. There is only one diva present on any shoot of his and it's always him. No exceptions.

So he knows when he summons her, she has been ready and waiting for a while.

Bernard begins describing the set up to Cee Cee. She is terrified when she sees the height of the tower but is wise enough to conceal it with humor,

"Geez, Bernie, put me on a mountain, why don't you?" She hopes Bernard does not smell her fear. She can smell it.

"You can do it, doll. It will be empowering for you and zhat, ironically, is zhe underlying zheme of zhis commercial," his words dripping in overemphasized French inflection.

"How so?" she asks.

"Well my darling, you are playing zhe part of a modern Rapunzel. You approach zhe tower and look up. Aha! You see yourself looking back down, helpless. Oh,my! You start to scale zhe tower like a rock climber as zhe camera closes in on zhe Hypothesis logo on zhe jeans."

"Bernie. You mean my butt," Calliope smarts off.

"Yes, darling. Zhat is where zhe jeans are. When you reach you, you are not zhere. And zhen zhe words running across zhe screen will say:

You don't need a man or a hairstyle.

Save yourself.

Hypothesis Jean Company"

Calliope, impressed, returns, "Gotta' hand it to you. Pretty catchy."

"Go get dressed zhen." Bernard instructs her.

"Sure thing. I need five minutes." Cee Cee returns.

"You have two," Bernard snaps back.

"Nazi!!"

Bernard stands at attention and raises his right arm in German salute announcing: "Ya vohl!" It just sounds wrong with the heavy French accent.

Calliope dashes for a small green room inconspicuously placed south of the main dressing room. She opens her Luis Viton carry all and removes the thermos hiding in the bottom. Cee Cee unscrews the lid and places it on the side of a tiny sink. She reaches deeper into the bag and pulls out a long comb with a small section of teeth and an extra, long handle. She inserts the handle deep into her throat and tickles the back of her throat with the extension.

Helloooooo lunch.

Calliope's eyes begin to immediately water as the remnants of her previous meal escape the sanctity of her stomach. Her throat burns from the acid she is forcing up as she positions her mouth just so over the opening on top of the thermos. She fills the vacuum to capacity and returns the lid. The thermos insulates the sound of this covert and humiliating act. Calliope cannot risk the acoustics of vomit landing in a toilet bowl, models get marked by their weaknesses. She pulls a towel from a holder on the wall and wipes any evidence from her lips. She then returns the comb and the thermos, heavier now from the vomit, to the abyss of her bag.

Nice to see you again. Don't take it personally, you were delicious.

She is mentally speaking to the quinoa flavored vomit that is escaping her nose. Wiping it away, she reassesses her appearance in the mirror. Usually Calliope avoids the mirror, ashamed of her condition. Images of starving children flood her mind as she forces up perfectly good food.

"I've got this down to a Science," she tells no one but herself.

Calliope returns to the set with long, curled hair extensions wearing a romantic, ecru lacy blouse and a tight pair of Hypothesis jeans. She takes one look at the tower and states:

"Ok, fellers, let's get this road on the show!" She is frightened half out of her mind.

The Meat of the Matter

Vinnie, satiated and bloated with Bolognese and stiff Italian bread, kicks back his tweed Lazy boy to a fully prone position. He lifts the remote control from the improvised table to the left. The table is an antique pickle urn with a decapitated stereo cabinet serving as its cover. He powers on his television set, thirty-two inches, no frills. Flipping through the channels, he pauses briefly on a hockey game and then continues clicking until he reaches an episode of Forensic Files. Vinnie considers this job training.

Research. I needs to know what to be careful of in my bidness.

Chuckling to only himself, he is amused at the thought that cable television is gracious enough to provide him with the information he needs to make a clean kill. To Vinnie, it's a veritable manual on assassination, although he is sure that is not the intent.

Tonight's episode is one he has seen repeatedly about the Gatorade, the poison and the unhappy wife with a boyfriend. Vinnie watches it in zombie mode and returns to Spark's Steakhouse and his meeting with Boss.

The olds pulls slowly in front of the iconic restaurant and pauses just left of the door. Carmine turns to Vinnie who is still seated in the back and says,

"Out you go, Weasel."

"Only the old guys call me that. Thanks for the ride youse guys," Vinnie replies.

The boys nod their heads and wait for the old man to exit. Vinnie opens the door, pops his legs out and discovers he cannot push himself up.

"You okay man? Do you need help getting out?" Nicky asks him.

"Nah," Vinnie said as he waves them away, "it's just mileage."

Vinnie offers both men a small salute as he exits the car. A searing pain shoots from north to south across Vinnie's right knee causing him to stumble and land his leg hard on the curb. Embarrassed to be so disabled in front of the young uns', he waves it off as a pavement infraction, frowns at the ground and briskly walks as straight as his pain will allow him into the glass front door of Spark's.

The matre' d instantly acknowledges The Weasel and gives Vinnie a brief nod and his usual:

"Right this way, sir."

The gentleman leads Vinnie to a generous corner booth where Boss is sitting, forcing a piece of bruschetta into his mouth. Boss does not stand but flags Vinnie into the booth and continues to chew his tomatoey bread. Boss gestures with his left hand indicating he wants Vinnie to help himself.

Vinnie selects a small piece of Italian bruschetta bread, dips it deep into the balsamic glaze sweeping it left and right and then drowns it in his mouth. Despite the fear he is also swallowing at the time, his taste buds explode with the marriage of basil and garlic.

"Mmmmm," he murmurs, "It's always good here."

"That's why I let them stay in business, ha, ha!" Vinnie dutifully presents the pity laugh. He is diligent to camouflage the pity part, it is too dangerous. Boss is too dangerous. He is, in fact, lethal.

Vinnie studies his superior trying to dissect the purpose for this meeting or discover some sliver of intent in Boss' expression. The one thing any hit man wants is to know what's coming. And when. When is good, too.

Always the final authority, Boss speaks: "I took the liberty of ordering our food before you arrived so that we could get right down to business. I selected the panella and mushroom ravioli."

Vinnie nods in agreement because no one argues with the palate of the boss and he waits for the food to arrive. In moments, the waiter appears with a large bowl of ziti in butter sauce with a huge fork and spoon inserted in the center. He lowers it to the table and paints each man's plate with a heaping portion. Another waiter appears behind him with a large clay bowl of panella and another one filled with ravioli.

Boss waits until the panella is on a plate in front of him to disclose any information:

"Vincent. I am hearing many things about this business with Tommy," the overfed Italian begins. Vinnie does not respond but chokes down a hard swallow and tries to keep his expression even and his heart rate low.

Boss goes on, "Nicky and Carmine. They are young and they are stupid but they are loyal and strong. I don't expect you Vincent, forgive me, but at your age to keep up with Nicky and Carmine. You have the experience and a cool head for the jobs I assign to you. You always get it done. But Carmine and Nicky can be the ones now who get their hands a little soiled."

Boss gets right to the point, states his opinion and then business is finished. He is not accustomed to anyone presenting an argument. He says it, it is done. Period.

Vinnie is devastated as he questions,

"Boss, is youse losing faith in me?"

He is both wounded and confused. Vinnie is pushing his luck but Boss likes him so he overlooks the effort.

"No, Vincent, I am not. But hear me now. Every man must admit when he has reached his expiration and know it is time to back off. I need you right where you are. Holy Mother, Vinnie, you and me are walking down are final paths. We're no spring chickens and not as invincible as we once were. We cannot be kicking it old school with the state of our tickers. I just want you to take a more supervisory position on the next job, capisce?"

"I get youse meaning. Nicky and Carmine need to learn the ropes and I can teach them a knot or two," Vinnie responds.

"It's all I am asking of you," Boss continues, "now flag that waiter and get our check since we have sealed this arrangement with ravioli already."

Vinnie had barely lifted his right hand configured in the "come here" pose when the waiter serving the table assembles himself for service.

It is quite a privilege to feed a Weasel.

Jeff Surfing

Flip. Flip. Click. Smack. Flip. Click. Click. Jeff is home, channel surfing. He stops briefly on a repeat episode of *Dr. Oz.* It's an encore airing on a cable channel this weekend. A few syllables halt his search:

"...truly that is one of the concerning issues with our young people today. They are obsessed with social media. We have Iphones permanently attached to our hands. And even more disturbing, our youth are more interested in getting the perfect duck face selfie than the state of a nation fallen to such incredible vanity...."

Jeff answers his television set.

"Bud, the only thing wrong with the younger generation is we cannot compete with your nostalgia. In my day, we didn't... the swan song of the baby boomer."

Blanket statements annoy Jeff who is not that easily irritated.

Jeff tires of hearing his elder coworkers complain about the youth of today. He knows Dr. Oz can't hear him but he feels better defending his generation anyway.

Flip. Flip. Click. Flip. Flip.

"Buh,buh,buh Bengals. Bengals. Bengals. Bengals. Bengals and the Jets..."

"That's the ticket. I should've started there."

Jeff is comfortable. He is eating a meal and preparing to watch a football game. Jeff misses his favorite sport when he is out of town working on a tower site. It is the anniversary of 911 and he is celebrating Patriot's Day by himself. Cee Cee is working on her Hypothesis campaign and Jeff has just come off a nine day run to Louisiana. He is massively anticipating some quality time with his bride.

News Flash

"Good evening and welcome to the six o clock news. I'm Melanie Shaker."

"And I'm Ross Perkins."

"Tonight we have a breaking news item to bring you. This just in: model Calliope Cash has been severely injured in a fall today while preparing to kick off her new campaign for the designer of Hypothesis Jeans. Sources on site tell us that a 30 feet tower had been constructed to re-create the story of Rapunzel. Miss Cash apparently fell while ascending a tower and performing the expected duties of this particular shoot. We understand it was a unique set up with an element of risk involved for Miss Cash. We have a representative of Hypothesis on satellite imaging to give us further details. Go ahead Lucy."

"Yes, Ross, Melanie, this is Lucy Winchester on the set of the Hypothesis Jeans shoot in an undisclosed location here in New York City. I am standing with Bernard Baxter, the director of this project. Mr. Baxter, can you give us more details about the accident and the condition of Miss Cash?"

"As you can well imagine, we are all still traumatized over zhe events of zhe past hour. We were shooting Calliope on zhe tower as she ascended it in a pair of Hypothesis jeans. It was a loose reconstruction of Rapunzel and Calliope was climbing zhe tower instead of waiting inside it to be rescued. She was about halfway up zhe side when zhe plaster gave way under her foot and she screamed and zhen slammed her body to zhe ground. I was filming at zhe time and all I saw was her flying through zhe frame. It was horrifying. Completely horrifying. I will never be zhe same."

"Do you have any word on the condition of Miss Cash?" the reporter prodded him.

"Not as yet. She has been rushed to Mount Sinai hospital and she was not conscious when zhey took her but she was breazhing." Baxter answered.

Jeff's plate shatters on the cherrywood floor creating a collage of macaroni, green beans and chicken. A river of Mountain Dew flows rapidly beside it. In his rush, he fails to even properly close the door to their apartment.

Mt. Sinai, New York

Two glass doors creep open and Jeff sprints to the first counter he comes to, "I need to see about my wife," Jeff pleads to the receptionist.

"I will be happy to help you, sir. What is your wife's name?" the receptionist at the front desk inquires.

"Calliope Seaton, I mean Cash. Calliope Cash."

The receptionist looks up from her computer screen and says: "Very funny, sir. I really don't have time for your games this evening."

"I am not playing with you. I am Jeff Seaton. Calliope Cash IS my wife! Please can I just see her?" Jeff is beyond begging.

"Sure, you and about 3 million other men wish THAT were true." The look on her face speaks volumes.

Jeff, now pleading, "I have to see how she is, please believe me!"

"If she is your wife, then why didn't you accompany her in? Geez, the lengths you people go to for a glimpse of a celebrity. I will give you credit for boldness, though. I guess it didn't occur to you that it is a documented fact that Calliope Cash is not now, nor has she ever been, married. Good day, sir." The receptionist appears triumphant. Clearly she has done this before.

"Ok, listen. I know that you have no reason to believe me but I can prove it." Jeff scrolls back two years on his cell phone and locates a grainy photo of himself and his bride at their wedding. "See, there we are. Married."

The receptionist, now flustered, spews at Jeff: "Dear Lord, do I look stupid to you? Hmmpf. Photoshop."

Jeff, now exasperated as well as terrified, replies, "Look, I am desperate to see about my wife. I know it is hard to believe. Can you tell me if her agent brought her here today?"

"Sir that would be a HIPAA violation if I answer that question." Again, triumphant.

"Alright, look, her agent's name is Jerry Henry. Now, how else could I know that? Please just call upstairs to whatever floor you have her on and ask the staff if Jerry is here. He will vouch for me." Jeff is weary but persistent.

Still unconvinced, the receptionist reluctantly dials the ICU unit on the fifth floor.

  "Yes, this is Hilda in admissions. I have a man here claiming to be the husband of Calliope Cash. I know, I know, that's what I thought as well." Hilda rolls her eyes and cracks a microscopic grin.

The receptionist intentionally avoids eye contact with Jeff as if that disguises her amusement in any way.

  She continues: "We seriously do have to do that, for sure," popping her gum she looks less than anxious to serve. "Listen, just for the sake of argument, can you see if there is a Mr. Henry, supposedly an agent hanging around up there…oh, he is. Can I speak with him, please? (after a brief pause) Yes, Mr. Henry, this is admissions. I have a..... (she places the receiver down and asks Jeff) what was your name again?"

"JEFF. JEFFREY DALE SEATON." He is losing his mind right now.

"a Jeff Seaton here who is....uh, huh.....umm hmm, yes, you have to be so careful these days. Of course, you have my complete discretion on the matter."

Hilda in admissions ends the call. Refusing to make eye contact now she announces: "Fifth floor, ICU. They will buzz you in."

Jeff doesn't hang around long enough to hold a grudge, he darts for the stairwell and takes the risers two and three at a time. He isn't even winded when he sees the number five and he crushes the door as he exits into the hallway. He quickly scans the signage and then turns left and sprints toward the ICU unit. As he approaches the landing that rises to the entry door, Jerry meets him halfway and Jeff falls onto his chest crying.

"Is she gone, Jerry? Is she gone?" Jeff pleads.

"No, buddy, she's not gone. But it doesn't look good." The words pierce Jeff and he collapses to his knees sobbing.

Jerry helps him to his feet and says, "Let me take you to your bride."

The anesthetic of the ICU is strong and overwhelming. If a concerned family member isn't scared enough, the smell and the leading down long, bleak corridors combine to place one in a state of complete panic before even glimpsing the patient. Jeff will not remember this walk any more than a condemned man can recall his trek. The trauma to him almost as serious as the trauma to his bride, though mostly internal injuries. He determines to stay in his right mind, to absorb all the information given to him so that he can be a proper spokesman for his model wife. It is his duty as her husband despite what he might find.

Calliope is attached to all sorts of gadgets and Jeff has seen enough episodes of *House* to decide that she is not breathing on her own. This fact alone destroys him but he holds it in well. Jerry speaks first.

"The doctor has her on life support but she is breathing ten times per minute on her own. The tube is just an extra precaution until they can determine the extent of her injuries. So far, it seems to be a fractured pelvis and the coma has been induced."

"The news said she was unresponsive," Jeff counters.

"She is unconscious, but not unresponsive. The coma was induced in the case of traumatic brain injury," Jerry returns. Jeff hit the floor. He could hold it no more.

"Oh, Cee, Cee. Please come back to me." Jeff burrows a hole in his hands and fills them with his tears.

Jerry places one hand on Jeff's back and says, "Listen, it is serious but we need to stay positive for her. She can hear us now."

Jeff wipes his salty grief across his plaid American Eagle shirt and replies, "Of course, she can. I love you, honeybun. I am not leaving until you get up and leave out of here with me."

Calliope smiles.

"Did you see that? She smiled at me!!!! She heard me!" And now Jeff knows she will indeed walk out with him.

Dr. Fisher

Steven is remarkably calm when the news of his patient flies into his office. He retains his coolness while in the presence of Miss Honeycut simply stating to send a card and reschedule her next appointment. Inside, he is churning with one statement.

Calliope Cash is in a coma.

Steven is not clear on what it means as far as her retaining memories of her sessions with him.

Will she revisit each appointment? Will she uncover that she has been seeing me for almost nine months now?

Steven is so thorough and conscientious, he even suggests to Calliope that each subsequent appointment is the first so that she cannot recall what he has actually done with her and in fact she has no recollection of anything but her initial contact with him. It is sinister. He is sinister. His name could have been Simon Bar.

Dr. Fisher is certainly concerned that her hypnosis might manifest itself. All of his concern is at the possibility of his exposure, he cares very little for his patient. She is but a puppet to him, a beautiful specimen at his disposal. He will be reticent to lose her services but not heart broken by any stretch. Steven wears narcissism the way cheap women wear make-up. In thick layers.

Sinister. I like that word and I wear it well. Three beautiful syllables expressing a deeper turn than just bad boy. It suggests intellect and motive and impeccable planning. Like a supervillain. I am Hypno Man, do my will. I wonder how I would look in a cape, not some faggot red like Superman but perhaps a deep grey or purple, something sleek and scary and intimidating.

There is no one else like me. These imbeciles are fortunate to even share air with me much less benefit from my brilliance. So what if she does remember our sessions? Hypnosis is not accurate and I can explain away any memory she does have as false and concocted. I am too smart for any of them. They will never catch me.

Steven's obsession with power held him tight like a bungee cord to a free jumper and he is overcome with adrenaline each time he commands one of his puppets.

I love the power. I am their god and they worship me. It does not matter that I orchestrate that worship, worship on any level is power. They are mindless entities bowing to my every suggestion.

It amazes me how clever I am. Calliope tasted me in her mouth after our last session and I was brilliant:

"CALLIOPE GRACE!"

"I'm awake," the sleepy puppet reported.

Cee Cee was smacking her mouth and trying to clean off her tongue.

"Doctor Fisher, my mouth is dry and pasty. Is that normal?" Calliope tasted something but attached no significance to it.

"Yes, Miss Cash. Many of my past patients have reported the symptoms of a dry mouth immediately following a session. It is perfectly normal, no need to concern yourself."

Damn, I am good.

Sessions

Vinnie

Vinnie enters the outer office of Dr. Fisher. Ms. Honeycut buzzes him through.

Steven looks up from his computer screen at Vinnie as he enters.

"How's it hangin", Doc?"

"I am well, Mr. Castana. Please take a seat."

Vinnie selects the same seat he chooses for every appointment. He has pretty much peed on it, marking his territory and now it is his.

Steven continues, "Tell me how things have been for you lately. Any more episodes?"

"Well, Doc, that's the thing, youse see. I haven't had many attacks since youse been putting me under, but I have times I can't recall where I went or maybe all that I did."

"I see. Tell me more." If Steven is concerned, his face is hiding it.

"The other day I went to confession with Father Frankie and it was after I had that meeting with Boss. I remember the meeting and I remember the confession, but everything in between is fuzzy. I didn't get home until way into the evening and Analisa was angry with me. I could not tell her about my whole day because I could not remember it. Then I located some coconuts in my pocket. Analisa loves those coconuts."

"That was a thoughtful move on your part."

"Yeah, but Doc, that's where it gets a little nuts. I don't have no recollection of purchasing those coconuts for her. Am I losing it, or what?" Vinnie is displaying a fear Steven did not recognize.

"No, Mr. Castana, your sanity is intact. But I am aware of rare cases where hypnosis of a patient can cause memory lapses on the conscious side."

"There you go again." Vinnie tells him.

"Oh, yes. Let's see, layman's terms. Sometimes going into the mind can make other things go out. Like an exchange system, but only trivial items are misplaced. You will know and recognize all the people in your life but you may not recall a trip to the store or the plot of a movie you went to see. Do you understand?"

"I think so. Can you go in and fix it?"

Vinnie looks desperate as he pleads for Steven's help. He is desperate. He is considering Analisa.

What will she think of all this?

"I can give it a go. Let's make an attempt. Lie down on the couch and relax and we will begin."

The blood races through Vinnie from the top of his head to the soles of his feet. The Timex watch on his wrist ticks away 29 minutes.

"It's hot, Doc. Is it supposed to be so hot?" Vinnie questions his physician.

Dr. Fisher turns to face his subject and says,

"Yes, Mr. Castana. All is well. You have done an excellent job today."

"Whatever youse say…." Vinnie trails off.

Five Hours and Fifteen Minutes Later

Vinnie enters Dr. Fisher's office. Miss Honeycut buzzes him through but is puzzled as to why he needs a second appointment within the same day.

He must be a REAL nut case.

Vinnie is still under hypnosis and Steven's control from his appointment earlier in the day. Dr. Fisher is testing the waters to measure how long his subject/puppet can sustain a state of trance.

So far, Vinnie has defied all the odds and is shattering any recorded standard. Dr. Fisher is ecstatic with this result.

Steven addresses his patient,

"Now Mr. Castana, let us return to earlier today, five hours ago, when you were talking with me about being called to have lunch with your boss. Do you recall this conversation?"

"Do I? Youse know, Doc, I never been that scared before. Thought for sure my number was up. Seems it weren't no real sichy-ation,persay. Boss just wanted to tell me what a good job I done with Tommy." Vinnie is animated as he relays his day.

"Did you experience any palpitations or blackouts before or during this meeting?" Steven asks.

"In the Olds on the way over, I had a panic attack. I started to sweat and fell over in the back seat until Nicky smacked me back into myself. And my heart was racing when I got to Sparks Steak House, but since I ain't never known the boss to buy a guy his last meal, my adrenaline took a dive and I managed to stay upright for the whole meeting."

Steven is feverishly taking notes and so Vinnie gives him a minute to get things together. Then Steven begins to explain the process to Vinnie.

"Mr. Castana, I want to work a bit on curbing your anxiety now, so I want you to repeat after me:

"My heart is in rhythm and I can calm myself."

Vinnie repeats,

"My heart, it's in rhythm and I can calm myself."

"Now say it again," Dr. Fisher instructs. Vinnie repeats again,

"My heart it's in rhythm and I can calm myself."

Steven, now convinced that Vinnie is fully under his control, instructs him further.

"Mr. Castana, you will have no memory of your earlier appointment with this office today. You will have only the memory of this session and you will feel satisfied with the results. I want you to return now to 15 minutes ago when you walked into this room."

"How's it hangin", Doc?" Vinnie greets the good doctor as if it is the first time he has seen him today.

"Ah, very good, Mr. Castana. Now I want you to feel your heart slowing, your body calming itself. You are in control. You have all the power."

"I have the power...." Vinnie repeats.

"At the mention of your name, you will awaken with no memory of anything that has occurred besides our last five minutes here in this office."

In a loud and commanding voice, Steven almost shouts:

"VINCENT CARMINE!"

And Vinnie wakes up. His eyelids flutter up and he blinks hard twice.

"What happened?" Vinnie blinks hard as he asks the question.

"Your therapy happened." Fisher replies nonchalantly.

Rubbing his eyes with both hands, Vinnie asks: "How'd I do?"

"I would say you are an excellent candidate for this type of therapy," Steven answers him.

Vinnie chuckles, "Happy to have youse vote, Doc."

"You are nothing if not amusing, Mr. Castana," the doctor states.

"Eh, Doc, youse can call me Vinnie." The mob man is getting comfortable.

"Very well. Do you have any further questions for me?" Dr. Fisher inquires.

"Yeah, I do. How's come I can't remember any of this?" Vinnie queries him.

"Because it is working, Vinnie."

For me, anyway.

Steven at Home

Steven turns the key into his elaborate home giving no thought to the destruction at his hands. It amuses him, really, that his puppets are so gullible and susceptible to parlor tricks. Calliope is still lying in a bed at Mt. Sinai, but he has no real affection for her.

His lust for her is attached to his ability to control and humiliate her privately. Steven has no remorse for his actions. Calliope owes it to him. How dare she look like that? His narcissistic nature allows him to skirt all responsibility.

Calliope is more amusement than muse. He can get what she gives him from any number of women, he just loves holding the power button in his hand. He is proud of himself, arrogant even. And he loves the baby talk.

Dr. Fisher strides toward the great room, verbally commands the stereo to play Bach and falls into an overpriced piece of furniture, artistic and functional. He is thinking of Calliope just now.

She is my Barbie doll and I get to undress her.

The sad fact remains that Steven is not sexually attracted to his model friend. Truth be known, he is closer to asexual. He has even entertained the idea of loaning her out but it involves too many others and things can get muddy quickly. He is not a big fan of witnesses. It is not her beauty that arouses him, but rather her submission. He can command her to bark and she will. The magnitude of that kind of control is overwhelming and gratifying. He hungers for the godness of it.

Now with Vinnie, it is a whole different story. Steven's safe is quickly filling up with cash. Dr. Fisher does not need the money Vinnie is skimming for him. He has all he could ever spend sitting in an account in the Caymans as well as numerous liquid and real assets in town. He does not like Vinnie's cocky little street attitude and the layered threats Vinnie has laid at his feet thinking the doctor isn't wise to it. He is setting Vinnie up in self-defense. He knows of several colleagues who have treated wise guys and ended up with a concrete pedicure. Steven has no intention of letting this happen so he is working Vinnie up good and letting the dogs eat each other. He feels it is just a matter of time before they will catch and execute him but it is either him or Steven. And Steven is too narcissistic to take one for anyone else.

And PJ, well that's just fun.

That pretentious little Christian popping in here and trying to do the "right" thing because she is so consumed with guilt. Why? Because she was real for a minute and lusted after someone besides her husband? I showed her and her precious Cyrano what happens when you think you are too good for any one sin. I sent her head first into it. What a pitiful waste of all that moral turpitude. I almost can't wait to put her back under and get the details of that one. This is my private puppet show and I the master puppeteer.

Dr. Fisher reaches deep into the wine cabinet seated next to his reclinable art and pulls up a cold bottle of Dos Equis. He twists off the cap and sucks it slowly into his throat. He savors the smoothness of the drink and the satisfying temperature of this hops concoction. He takes the long neck of the bottle deep into his throat and whispers out loud:

"I know what's next for you too, Barbie doll."

Consequences

Mt. Sinai

Jeff is sitting by Calliope's side as he has for the past three days. She awakened forty-eight hours prior, sleepy and unable to recall much of the accident. Her memory is slowly and consistently returning now and each time his pretty returns to him, she returns to her right mind as well.

The doctor is supposed to come with an update today but she was supposed to be here yesterday and the day before so Jeff refuses to hold his breath for any sign of her. Most of Calliope's initial care occurred before Jeff had any awareness of her injury and so he has yet to speak to anyone but the nursing staff who dutifully keep singing,

"She should be here sometime today, sir."

It is simply the robotic response of a nameless nurse who is clearly covering for someone else.

And so what do you do? Scream and throw things so they have a reason to toss you out or sit dutifully and wait for information that one would think was a state secret?

And they say this is a great hospital.

Calliope coos in her sleep. Jeff loves it when she does that. It just proves to him that she really is his baby doll. She stirs slowly, stretches and sighs fluttering her unmade eyes open.

"Hi bub," she greets him.

"Hey, doll. What's up pup?" he plays with her.

"I don't know. You tell me. Has Dr. Disappearance Act showed yet?" she sleepily asks him.

"Nope." Jeff answers her.

"Nurses still covering for her?" Cee Cee asks.

"Yep."

"Hmmmm. Maybe we can be so evasive when they send us the bill. Or prorate it according to her bedside appearances or lack thereof," Calliope smiles back.

Jeff laughs and says: "I like the way you think, woman."

Calliope goes on, "I had the weirdest dream."

Jeff replies, "Let's hear it."

"It was odd. I had strings on my arms like I was being worked by someone else. I don't know like God, maybe? Anyway, there was freaky circus music and I couldn't move my arms but like a puppeteer or something was moving them for me and saying:

"Good girl, good girl."

And there were creepy clown faces but that's the strangest part because I have never had an issue with clowns and I worry about idiots who do. So even the fear was not accurate. I need to write that one down."

Jeff returns, "Well, honey, you probably do feel puppeted. These nurses have turned you, plugged you, stuck you and fed you with a tube. That dream makes perfect sense to me."

"I guess. What's for supper?" Calliope asks.

"They haven't come yet," Jeff answers.

"You may have to make a burger run," she quips.

"I will, you know that," Jeff offers with a smirk.

A charge nurse enters the room. She smiles at Jeff and addresses Calliope,

 "Well, how are you feeling today, Ms. Cash?"

"Pretty good, I think. When is din din?"

"They should bring lunch around soon. Dr. Abraham will be doing her rounds on this floor momentarily. She will want to speak with you."

 Jeff looks at Calliope. Calliope looks at Jeff. Neither one was buying it.

"OK," they report in unison.

The nurse checks Calliope's machines and places a blood pressure cuff on her left arm. She watches as the machine does most of her work and taps the result into a handheld device that replaces the prehistoric patient's chart. She smiles once again and exits the room with no parting pleasantry beyond her expression.

Calliope is just about to comment on her bedside manner or lack thereof when Dr. Ada Abraham enters the room. Dr. Abraham extends her right hand to Calliope and says: "I am the attending physician, Dr. Abraham. I am here to discuss your situation with you."

Calliope couldn't help herself. She blurts: "I thought you were a myth. Sort of like Big Foot."

Dr. Abraham ignores the attempt to both humiliate and amuse her. She has seen this before. Many times. No one really gets how many demands are placed on her time and she never feels the need to elaborate on it. It is too much like apologizing and that is the one thing she never does.

"I need to ask you some questions of a sensitive nature. Would you like me to ask your spouse to exit the room?"

"No, he's good," Calliope responds.

"OK then. Let's begin. Do you feel safe in your home?" The doctor asked.

"Yes, of course. Why would you ask me that? I was injured on the job!" Calliope is offended.

"Well," the doctor continued, "it is normally a routine question but in this case you also have an injury that is not explained by the fall," Dr. Abraham clarifies.

Jeff pipes in: "What injury are you talking about? The broken pelvis? They told us they decided it wasn't broken after they looked at the x-ray."

"Mr. Cash...."

"Mr. Seaton." Jeff corrects her.

"Mr. Seaton, the pelvis is intact. We have confirmed that with the images. Calliope has significant anal tearing. There is considerable damage to the rectum. We do not ever see that with a fall over ten feet."

141

Jeff falls back into his chair stunned. Calliope's mouth drops open and her face goes rice white. Neither one can explain or process what has just been laid there.

Jeff speaks first. "I don't understand. We don't do that. How could this....?" And he looks at Calliope, frantically searching for an explanation.

"Hey, I have no idea. You are my only...." This is too much for either one to figure out in a second's notice and that is all they are given before the next revelation.

The doctor speaks again, "The good news is the fetus is still viable."

Jeff's head turns. Calliope's head turns. In unison, they reply, "The what is what?!"

Calliope adds, "I am pregnant?"

"I take it you did not know," Dr. Abraham answers. "You are approximately 16 weeks."

The pregnancy news trumps the anal tearing which they will return to later.

Jeff screams, "Sixteen weeks!! Calliope!!"

"Jeff, I swear, I didn't know! Dr. I am bulimic. I vomit all the time without attaching any more significance to it than that was lunch..."

"This is a disturbing piece of information. Bulimia Nervosa can have serious consequences for a fetus." Dr. Abraham is condescending as she delivers this piece of information. And pious.

Jeff rescues her quickly, "She is seeing someone about it and has been for almost a year."

Calliope aghast replies, "Jeff, don't lie for me. I AM seeing someone but I have only had two appointments so far."

Now they have something else to discuss later.

Consequences

Preparations

PJ cuts herself shaving, curses mildly, *(shit)* and finishes her bath. She loves it when Brad leaves for work and now that both kids are out of the house, she can relish her hot water refuge. It is all she does for herself. Except fantasize about Cyrano. She cannot understand why after three sessions with Dr. Fisher that her desires are still so close to the surface. She wants to NOT want him. She is grateful this reputable physician has even agreed to take her on but she is starting to wonder if perhaps she is not susceptible to hypnosis. Nothing has really changed. Peyton feels an amplification of her affections, if possible, wanting him more.

When the water turns tepid, PJ dries herself on towels that are almost too soft and heads into the bedroom. Opening her closet, she peruses its massive contents feeling guilty as she does about her thoughts of another.

Brad treats me like a queen. But then most members of royal family have affairs. Stupid way to justify that, I am nowhere near royalty.

PJ selects a nice outfit, a blue jean skort, frilly top with beige lace and a pair of matching sandals from Macy's. She admires her outfit in the mirror remembering when she worked at the mall in her teens and how she always could put two things together and make them look great. Today, she does indeed look smashing and all she is planning to do is shop at Kroger to purchase a few missing items for her dinner menu.

PJ finishes primping and priming in the couple's bathroom just off the master bedroom. She surveys her face upon completion deciding she doesn't look too much worse for the wear. She tops it off with her favorite shade of pink lipstick, grabs her keys and cell phone and walks to the door.

PJ starts up the Buick and turns on the oldies rock station. <u>Carry on My Wayward Sun</u> erupts from the speakers. She sings every word as if Kansas' last concert had been yesterday. It amuses her that she remembers every word, pause and riff.

"Our music was hands down the best. No contest," she declares to the empty air in her vehicle. She puts the car in drive and sails west to the nearest Kroger.

Upon arriving at the store, she exits her car, pushes the locking mechanism, listens for the beep-beep and moves toward the grocery carts. She selects the larger one, because she knows the road to hell is paved with good intentions and she is very likely to purchase much more than what she really needs to this day.

As she turns down the health food aisle, she sees him. Cyrano in the flesh. He does not see her yet and she battles herself as to whether she should emerge and expose her presence or cower on and out the door.

What do I do? Is this my chance to find out if it's me?

Her heart rumbles within her chest. PJ feels every hair standing on its end. She settles on walking coyly by and pretending not to recognize him-forcing him to make the first move. First mistake.

Nervously, PJ slowly maneuvers the buggy closer to where he is standing, reading the back of a bag of wheat germ. Number two.

Cyrano looks up from his wheat germ and instantly recognizing PJ says,

"You have some nerve, Peyton."

With that, he slams the package of wheat germ back onto the counter and storms away.

PJ stands immobile, wounded and confused. She had no idea he knows who she even is (*on this issue, PJ was never sure*) or more importantly, what she has done to illicit such a reaction. For what seems like much longer than just a moment or two, she will not move, cemented to the hallowed ground where she has been verbally crucified. After the initial sting wears off, she quickly gathers herself and pursues her attacker. PJ watches him in the checkout lane, then works her way around him and walks outside the store to wait for his exit.

Her mind is racing and nothing makes any sense.

What did I do? Is he a mind reader? So far, everything has just been a fantasy, I have not revealed any of it to anyone except my doctor and he wouldn't….

Cyrano exits the Kroger and pushes his half full buggy to a Ford Fusion at the far left of the lot. PJ follows in close pursuit. After he loads half his purchase, she approaches him once again. The look of disgust that crosses his face makes PJ cringe so she quickly declares,

"I am sorry but I have no idea what I have done to you."

Cyrano stops what he is doing, turns to face her and says, "You can't be serious right now."

"I am. As a heart attack. Please tell me how I have offended you and I will apologize and make it right, I promise."

PJ is desperately seeking answers to this puzzle.

"I don't know what little game you are playing with me because I didn't even speak to you in high school but this little soul mate garbage and you assaulting me and then playing dumb blonde doesn't wash with me. I ain't no typical guy, sweetheart." Cyrano is an angry poet right now.

"I assaulted you?? When? This is the first time I have laid eyes on you since high school. What in hell are you talking about?"

PJ is not able to process what he is saying. She is too mortified. And devastated. And everything in between. All of it, all at once. A storm of humiliation brewing on the parking lot of the local Kroger.

There is something about her conviction and the confusion in her expression that convinces him to explore this further.

"Are you saying you do not remember coming to my house under the guise of being lost, practically inviting yourself in, and then jumping my bones as soon as the door closed?" Cyrano questions her, his voice dripping with thick repulsion.

PJ blushes and begins to weep. "I do not. Please help me figure this out. Can I buy you a cup of coffee, somewhere public, and you tell me the rest? Please. I swear I don't have any idea what you are talking about right now. Please." PJ is pleading now.

Cyrano looks at this pitiful, repentant, clueless creature before him and feels a minute stirring of compassion. "Ok, but only ONE cup. And you better behave."

Consequences

Vinnie in the Basement

Boss is stewing. He has known Vinnie all his life and now he is putting his good friend's name on a work order.

Whatever is going on with Vincent, it is affecting his ability to be trusted. Quite unacceptable.

Despite the necessity of this task, it is testing the boss. He likes Vinnie. Hell, he loves him.

Later

The two hitmen hear the rumble in the trunk but are familiar with this type of situation and so they are immune to the noise.

"I just can't believe it. Vinnie. Of all the guys. Vinnie."

"I get it. Or I mean, I don't get it either. He is such a stand-up guy and hell, I even like him. It might hurt a bit to do this tonight. But I'll get over it. If you can't get over stuff in this job, you ARE the next job."

"Right you are, my brother. Still can't believe we got Vinnie the Weasel in the back."

The dark sedan slows and Vinnie rolls up against the back of the seat. He feels a dark drop in his stomach when the car stops. He knows it won't be long before his heart follows suit. His confusion is the main issue this evening. Even as he lies hog-tied in the trunk of the sedan, he is stumped as to what betrayal he is being punished for this night. He does not even vaguely recall any infraction on his part and thinks perhaps his number has just come up. He knows too much. He thought about this moment many times and had long ago decided to die with dignity. No pleading. No begging. No hitting his knees. No matter what the plans are for his destruction. He will go out like a man. No way he wants Analisa to hear it happened any other way. This is the last husbandly thing he will do for her. Give her a good memory of a noble death not some whining ninny begging for a life he cannot save at this point. Vinnie is all boy.

Vinnie strains to hear the muffled voices and the squeaky sound of the passenger door opening. The driver's side door follows soon behind. He flinches as the key turns in the trunk lock, snapping and then slowly the lid is lifting. He looks no worse for the wear considering the lengthy ride and he immediately recognizes the location. The warehouse on fifth. Good call, boys. No one will ever hear anything or find remains. The warehouse on fifth is backed up against the river. The boss purchased it on purpose for disposal of undesirable material. Tonight, that material is Vinnie.

The boys reach in a little too gingerly and lift Vinnie from his temporary tomb. They escort him down two flights into an abandoned room with a small, cheap metal chair in the center. Spread across the oily floor, is a large piece of clear plastic sheeting along with several smaller pieces beside it. The chair is centered in the middle of the largest piece.

Well, this is what I figured. They are taking me out in pieces. Fish bait.

He tries not to show fear and he is doing well on the outside, but his anxiety is raging inside with concern about the actual method of his demise.

Please don't let me pass out, he consoles himself. Ain't this where Tommy bought it? I hope this is fresh plastic. No man should die in another chump's death stain.

The boys sit Vinnie in the cheap chair and swagger to an attached office with a dirty, glass observation window.

I guess Boss has box seats for this.

Vinnie pinches back his urine.

After about an hour, because boss knows the anticipation of one's death is way worse than the actual death, boss swaggers out and approaches Vinnie, still seated.

"Vinnie, how long have I known you, my friend?" Boss presses him.

"Boss, youse know how long. Since we was boys." Vinnie is desperate to maintain his heart rate.

"Vinnie, in all those years have you considered me your friend?" Boss is acting cool and professional.

"Youse know the answer to that one, too." Vinnie is just answering the question.

"You crackin' on me?" Boss looks annoyed.

"No, sir just statin' the facts." Vinnie doesn't figure on having anything else to lose at this point.

"Well, Vinnie, I am confused. If you and I have a history and a long one at that, what possessed you to steal from me, your friend for all this time."

Boss is looking Vinnie straight in the eyes, anticipating his response. The look on Vincent's face is real. He has no idea what Boss is talking about. Boss notes Vinnie's confusion and anxiously awaits his reply.

"Boss, I ain't got no idea what youse is talking about." Boss almost believes him.

"Vinnie, it's me. Ante up." Boss continues.

"Boss, I'm for real here." Vinnie is more confused than scared at this point.

"Boys, load the tape." Then boss steps back from the action for a bit, still determined to resolve the issue.

The boys emerge from the office pushing a rusty white metal cart with an older television sitting on the top. A long extension cord is attached to one end and a DVD holder is lying beside the set. The larger of the two men stand behind Vinnie while the smaller man inserts the disc and pushes play.

The DVD shows surveillance of the counting room. The counting room is boss' money management arena. In this place hundreds of thousands of dollars are counted and then laundered to various locations. The tape is routine until the seventh minute when

Vinnie enters and exchanges pleasantries with the five men counting out twenties, fifties and hundreds.

Nicolo is seated at the head of the table, followed by Marcario, Angelo, Freddy and Michael. Nicolo begins by passing large duffle bags down the table to the other men who are seated in succession. Angelo snubs out his cigar, unzips the first duffle and begins removing bundles of twenties and fifties. He stacks them awkwardly on the table. The other men follow his lead and in just a few moments, the table is a skyscraper of cash.

Vinnie watches with great interest as he holds no recollection of ever entering the counting room. He is not completely sure it even exists. The experience for him is truly out of body and he is just as stunned as the boss was the first time he watched the footage. Vinnie leans in closer to the television set as if improving his view will change the result.

In the video, Vinnie slinks over to the end of the table and takes a seat near the vault. None of the counters appear to be distraught over Vinnie's presence. They, too, would have never suspected him to be a thief.

After he sits down, the tape is self-explanatory. Vinnie is clearly pocketing cash when the men are distracted by their counting. He places several bundles in his coat pockets and down inside his socks. There is no way to know exactly how much he lifts, but it appears he has taken about four bundles of hundreds at approximately 10,000 per bundle. Forty thousand dollars. That's what Vinnie's life is worth.

Tower Time

Jeff adjusts his left hip in the recliner provided by the hospital. He imagines it is closer to some primeval torture device or an insurance plan for the facility to maintain a steady stream of business. He gazes upon his model wife as she sleeps, unmade, and as stunning as she ever could be. He prefers her without makeup as he never sees her need for it. Calliope is sleeping quietly with that occasional coo. He loves the little intricacies that they are still discovering about one another. And he loves that she is his. He knows that most people would imagine their love is simply a superficial, chemical attraction but his heart and hers know better. He will sit here, at her side, forever if needed. He knows Calliope would do the same and in fact she already proven her reciprocal devotion to him just one year earlier…

Foster, Kentucky

The Verizon Tower 2175

It was sweltering. The kind of hot you peel off at the end of the day. The kind of heat that cemented your shirt to your skin.

Jeff was sent with Bernie and Harold to inspect Tower 2175 in Foster and to repair the light casing at the peak of the site. It was decided that Jeff would scale the 300-foot metal Leviathan, Harold would ground crew and Bernie would run rope.

Jeff, Bernie and Harold slowly drove to Tower 2175, parked the vehicle for Thompson Tower Service and exited the truck. Jeff walked to the side of the truck and began opening doors. He retrieved his helmet, safety harness and other climbing gear. Jeff attached his safety harness to his waist, double checked the strings on his climbing boots and quickly prepared himself for a 45-minute ascent. He double and triple checked each carabiner for its strength. It still amazed him that a tiny piece of steel could be responsible for holding him to a tower even in high winds and foul weather. Jeff sat down at the tower base and consumed two bottles of water. He strapped six more to his side and prepped his mind for the climb ahead. After strapping on his helmet he called out to Harold:

"I'm up and at'em."

"Ok, climber go ahead," Harold responded.

Bernie grabbed Jeff's tools and the items needed to make the repair on the tower light seated at the peak of the metal mountain. He then grabbed a nosebag and the rope and prepped it to be lifted to the upper work site. Bernie opened a door on the left side of the truck and selected the halogen bulbs needed for the repair which came in two sets of three flash tubes. He carefully placed them on top of the tools and other equipment.

"Too bad these lights aren't housed in the middle!" he quipped to Jeff.

"Maybe we should suggest that, Bern!" Jeff teased in return.

"Boys, it's a scorcher. The thermometer on the fence read 108 degrees," Harold offered up. They all knew that meant it was a much higher reading up top.

"Well, we've done worse for ourselves," Jeff replied.

"Indeed, my friend. Indeed, we have," Harold returned wondering as he did if the company had any clue how close they had come to buying the farm and on how many occasions. The tower itself was a dangerous undertaking but his crew was talented and trained. And they did not take crazy chances. Every "t" was crossed, every "i" was dotted. They understood the magnitude of their profession and they each had people at home.

But the incredible heat was another story. That factored with the wind current could muss up even the most letter perfect job. It was a grave situation when a climber succumbed to a heat emergency and it was an even graver situation to get that technician down. And that had never happened until this day.

With the ground temperature at 108, the tower temp could rise to as high as 115 degrees. Jeff, now dressed with his helmet attached, approached 2175. Jeff pulled the carabiner from his safe climb device and hooked his waist onto the steel cable running parallel to the tower ladder and began to rise himself to the top. The line was a backup device for any misstep and was designed to give only six inches in the case of a fall or slip.

At thirty feet, Jeff began to feel a bit of fatigue, so he stopped, hooked onto the ladder rung and reached around his back to retrieve a bottle of water. He thought it odd that he had only risen 30 feet before he needed to hydrate. At sixty feet, he repeated the process and again at 90 and so on until he had safely risen.

Man, it's really hot and I am taking in a lot of fluid.

Forty minutes later, he was safely seated, had consumed three additional bottles of water and two Gatorades and commenced to repair the tower's beacon. Jeff maneuvered himself off the ladder after disconnecting his lifeline. He free climbed to the outside of the tower and hooked back in to the bar in front of him.

Jeff reached around to his back side and removed the rope suspended from his waist. He hooked it to the top of the tower and then tied a crescent wrench to one end and lowered it end over end down to Harold.

As Harold was sending up the nosebag on the line Jeff had sent to him, Jeff drank another water and surveyed the view. He could see the AA highway and farms full of deer that looked more like ants from 300 feet up. The trees always looked like broccoli and they reminded him of growing up in West Virginia hills where nothing was taken for granted. Nor wasted. He missed home.

Harold called over the radio. "Ground to tower."

"Go ahead."

"Accessories on the way up," Harold informed him.

"Thanks, man."

Jeff reached deep into the canvas nosebag scraping his hand on the leather bottom until he felt the lanyard. He removed the Y lanyard and attached the left carabiner to a bar tower left, the center D ring to a stationery carabiner on his vest just below the back of his neck, and attached the right carabiner to a bar on tower right. Having secured himself to freely move about the job, he disconnected the safe climb device from his waist and headed toward the beacon to begin the repair. The Y lanyard allowed Jeff to step from bar to bar on the tower top and move safely into position.

Jeff firmly turned and gently removed the housing panel on the strobe. He carefully placed the canopy to one side balancing it on the metal bars at the top. He reached deep into his nose bag for the proper wrench and retrieved it. He prepared to replace the light casing. He snapped in the two sets of flash tubes, buttoned it all back up and then lifted the cover to reseat the lantern. The lantern came to life as soon as the bulbs were seated so Jeff called for a ground test. The cover would not sit itself properly as the sealant had been destroyed. Jeff grabbed his radio from his side.

"Tower to ground, come in."

"This is ground, go ahead."

"Harold, I need some caulk to seal this casing. Can you rope it up, please? And can we field test this light? I think it just needed the new bulbs," Jeff informed him.

"Will do."

Harold walked to the facility building and flipped a switch. "Tower, are we good?"

"We are good. I'm closing her up," Jeff responded.

"10-4."

Jeff lowered the nosebag to the ground. Harold headed for the truck and located caulk sealant in the first door he tried. He placed the caulk in the nosebag and hoisted it the 300 feet necessary to Jeff. He did not hear from Jeff again until Jeff was hanging by an altogether different rope.

The climb and the repair took five hours and once completed, Jeff began to load his tools and prepare for his descent. He lifted his right arm and grasped the metal bar in front of him. His hand immediately began to cramp and closed his fingers around the bar for good. Jeff could not release his hold as the excruciating cramp began to migrate South and North at the same time. The pain was unbearable but the fear of falling to his death easily trumped it. He knew he could not get himself off the tower. He recognized his dire state as severe heat exhaustion because, as stated before, the tower technicians are a well-trained bunch. The only thing more painful than the body now betraying him was the call he knew he had to make to ground. Jeff used gravity to pull his hand from the tower and then sheer will to push the button on his radio.

This is bad. This is real bad.

"Ground." Jeff called.

"Go ahead." Harold responded.

"I'm in trouble. Body cramps."

That was all that needed to be said. Harold was a 32-year veteran in his field and he knew that Bernie was going up that tower and Jeff needed a rescue.

"Okay, man. Hang tight. We got ya'." Harold only hoped that Jeff believed him.

Harold sprinted to Bernie and started to prep the rescue rope. Harold ran to the truck, ripped open a door and pulled out a fisk descender. This was a double hole carabiner with a locking mechanism and a horn like that on a saddle seated at the top. Harold began to tie off the rope looping it in and out of the fisk descender to reduce the friction for the descent. This tiny rope and 6-inch piece of metal had to support the dead weight of two grown men. Neither one a light weight. Although time was of the essence, Harold was meticulous to string it correctly given the gravity of the situation all the while hoping that Jeff did not lose consciousness. It would be an entirely different rescue if he did.

Meanwhile, Jeff who had made his way to the ladder prior to the cramping was hydrating and anxiously awaiting Bernie's arrival.

Bernie prepared himself for his second climb of the day having ascended half-way up earlier to unsnag a line.

Bernie was almost ready to climb when Harold gave him a final instruction:

"Get our man down."

In the interim, Jeff was praying and drinking as much water as possible while Bernie made a 45-minute ascent in 27.5 minutes. He set an ascent record that day and now both climbers were at risk for heat stroke.

"Ground to tower." Harold called up.

"Tower, come back." Jeff responded.

"Jeff, you still good, man?" Harold asked him.

"I'm hangin' in. Harold?" Jeff weakly inquired.

"Yea,man?"

"Don't call Cee Cee until I am on the ground."

"Copy." Harold replied.

Jeff felt a quick relief as he watched Bernie's face rising in front of his.

"What's up?" Bernie asked him in jest.

"It ain't about up right now man, it's more about down!" Jeff returned now cramped and wrapped around a ladder rung.

"Well, let us see what we can do about that," Bernie declared.

Jeff released the carabiner mechanism that allowed him to lower himself 10-15 feet to reach Bernie. He used this technique twice until Bernie positioned himself to Jeff's left side and dropped into place below him. He reached for the safety rope that Harold had hoisted earlier and double-checked each mechanism. Bernie then pulled up the slack on the rope and wrapped it snugly around the horn at the top. Jeff hooked the rescue carabiner to a strong bar at tower top. Once the rope was rigged and ready, Bernie rested and took in some water. He hooked onto one end of the fisk descender, then to the boatsmen's chair from the D ring on the spreader bar. He was near ready to unhook himself from the safety of the tower, a move no techie ever wants to make, and hook onto a miniscule but strong safety line into one half of the fisk descender that will then suspend both men away from the structure. He removed Jeff's tool belt and other unnecessary items of weight and placed them at the top of the tower.

They are probably there to this day.

Bernie continued strapping Jeff to a separate carabiner into the "D" ring at the base of Jeff's neck and prepared to descend. Jeff was now dangling by the neck beneath Bernie as he prepared to release the rope on the fisk descender and slowly work it through the mechanism into a slow and treacherous descent. The push off was the most difficult move because there was no going back from detaching one's self from the tower. At that point, you either repel or plummet and no practice session of this maneuver can prepare a man to plummet.

Jeff's heart rate sat at 134 and Bernie's was just slightly lower. Jeff had managed to will himself to remain conscious so he was also able to communicate with Bernie on the way down and to help extend an arm pushing both men away from the structure as it widened on the descent.

Cautiously they began the 29-minute trip South. At seventy-five feet, Jeff told Bernie to stop and pour water on the fisk descender to keep the heat and the friction from compromising it. They would stop twice more before safely hitting ground. Upon reaching the ground, Jeff assumed a fetal position so Bernie could drop both legs safely on either side of his body.

The emergency medical personnel who had assembled themselves at the site during the two-and-a-half-hour rescue attempted to swarm Jeff but were held off by Harold until Bernie was safely down. Two paramedics helped Jeff to his feet and immediately placed him into an ambulance, rushing him to the local medical facility. Bernie was taken in a separate ambulance as a precaution.

Then Harold placed the call to Calliope.

Steven Thinks Things Through

Sometimes when I squint my eyes in the mirror, I see Sheldon Cooper. A steelier, more handsome version of course. Sheldon sans OCD, that idetic memory and annoying self-obsession. I am intelligent like he. Refined and educated like he. And I resemble him. Socially, I am light years ahead of Dr. Cooper.

Steven leans in closer to the mirror to examine the trident, his Achilles' heel. In truth it is a duodent, if there is such a thing, a two-pronged spear sailing across his retina interrupting the blue. It gives Steven's appearance an inherently evil twist and he despises it. His eyes are icy blue which means there is no disguising this devilish apparatus crossing his vision. He inserts dark brown contacts each day to mute the shape of his birth defect. It is the only flaw he will ever admit to having-a sinister wand of Satan sailing across his face.

Steven knows this aberration of his gene structure to be an outward sign of his inner demons and he prefers to keep his true self a little more tightly wrapped.

Dr. Fisher never thinks much about the patients he is treating. In truth, they are just a mortgage payment to him and he refuses to invest any empathetic nonsense on such a cause. He knows he is much more intelligent than any of them because he is slick enough to re-hypnotize each one before they leave his office so that they will not recall what he might have done to them or programmed in them for later.

He recognizes how brilliant it is to do it this way and he figures on never getting caught.

But Steven underestimates PJ and her desire to be a good person. And he is truly a fool to mess with the life of a mobster. With Calliope, and he knows this, he can pull off anything. She has too much to lose. And Calliope is highly skilled at keeping deep, dark secrets.

Then the voice he never listens to whispers:

And the transgressors will fall. Hosea 14

Rabbit Remembrance

Calliope's eyes flutter and then shut. Flutter. Shut. Flutter. Shut. She squints at the perilous sun ray piercing her hospital bed and splitting it like a log. She closes her eyes again for just a moment more and leans her head back into the pillow. Slowly she drinks in the sunny heat sighing as the sun paints first color, then texture in her lids. Reluctantly she opens them again and notices Jeff, cock-eyed and crooked sleeping in a chair. Instantly it transports her to Tower 2175 and that microscopic medical center where her husband lay recovering.

I think we got this "in sickness and in health" thing down, dear.

Calliope does not linger on the tower memory that still makes legitimate vomit well within her, instead she chooses to remember the tower story that is more theirs than anyone else's. She remembers how they met. She loves remembering this.

Calliope had just gotten a foot hold in the New York modeling scene. Until this time, she had not made enough money to even make rent and had been comped so many pieces of clothing she would never need to buy anything to wear ever again. It was exasperating to her how her face could show up in a magazine with a massive circulation, and she received goods instead of cash for her services. A girl's gotta' eat. It was this mindset that placed her deep in Amish country, in Lancaster, Ohio.

Cee Cee was working a location shoot for milk of all things. It was the one product she really didn't care for because she orally fixated on the phlegm that forms after drinking it. Which she almost never did. But the milk industry thought it would be so cute to put her in a huge field, with an Amish farm as a background, to glorify their thick, velvet liquid product. Cee Cee never mastered lying but she was an adequate saleswoman. Which is almost the same thing.

Jeff was on ground working on a tower sight about 100 yards away. He noticed a girl and the others working the location, but he was a guy, so he lost interest in it quickly. About halfway through the shoot, a piercing yet delicate scream filled the space between them. A primal utterance that echoed across the wheat fronds. Jeff had heard the same sound many times and knew exactly what it was but the noise was foreign to Calliope and so she investigated the source of the sound. She put a finger up to the director to indicate she would be right back and she walked about fifty yards away from the camera. When she found the injured rabbit, she had an immediate reaction. Calliope quickly bent down and cradled the pitiful creature in both hands. A look of great concern crossed her face but Jeff, who was watching her every move, never saw that beautiful look of concern. He saw her heart. Jeff fell in love with her at the precise moment. A nameless girl cradling a dying bunny.

Calliope knew the animal was probably fatally injured, but she continued to cup the tiny little body in her hands and say: "It will be ok, sweet thing. I will nurse you back to health."

She didn't even hear Jeff approaching until he said, "What have you got there?"

She looked up at him squinting against the sun. He was towering over her in his hard hat and climbing gear, covered in both sweat and dirt. He was wearing a motorcycle mask of filth on his face. She thought him beautiful.

"It's injured. I don't know what happened and I don't know how to help it." Cee Cee whimpered to him.

"Well, let me take a gander at it," Jeff offered.

Calliope handed the bunny over to him gingerly and Jeff received it the same way. He did a quick scan of its broken body by holding it up and surveying the undercarriage and sliding his hands left and right.

"You can't move it too much, his insides are all torn up," Jeff informed her.

"What do you think happened?" Calliope asked.

"Tractor. I've seen it lots of times. Rabbits are no match for a tractor and a farmer with bad eyes." Jeff returned.

"It's so sad. Is there anything we can do?" Calliope was pitiful, more wounded in a way.

Jeff answered, "Well, you can try to mend it. Wrap it up good in your scarf and keep it warm so it won't go into shock. On your way home, get an eye dropper and some Carnation milk and you can try to feed it. It will probably still die, though. Circle of life."

That was the moment Calliope fell in love with Jeff. It was the cadence of his voice and the compassion that came dripping off every syllable. He was just as concerned for her as he was for this tiny, furry charge of hers.

"Thank you so much. My name is Calliope."

"Nice to meet you Miss Calliope. My name is Jeff."

Each one gazed into the other's eyes and saw forever.

Coffee with Cyrano

PJ is following closely behind Cyrano as he drives the two blocks to the nearest Starbucks. He pulls in to the small strip mall and parks in the spaces up front near the door of the coffee shop. PJ pulls in beside him and exits her vehicle fumbling nervously with keys and her Kate Spade wristlet. They move together, but not together. PJ has no idea what she has done to offend Cyrano and she is careful not to spook him until she can find it out what it is. Cyrano, ever the gentleman, opens the door for Peyton and follows in behind her.

"I'm buying-what will you have?" PJ offers.

"Tall, blonde roast, black, please," he flatly delivers.

"Ok," she responds without her usual thought of how precisely one can order a stupid coffee these days. And also how much you learn about someone when they order it.

PJ walks briskly to the desolate counter, grateful for the ghost town atmosphere as she expects to be overwhelmingly embarrassed in a short time. She orders his blonde roast along with an iced green tea with five Splendas and waits for the barista to prep and shake her order. Cyrano finds a tiny table in the back by the restrooms and seats himself.

PJ retrieves the two beverages, mentally drinking the redolence of his steaming coffee and briefly regretting her green tea selection. Her heart is breaking speed records in her chest as she heads toward the table.

Cyrano takes a long, deep sip of his blonde and avoids eye contact with PJ. He speaks first.

"Thanks for the drink," he offers.

"It is my pleasure." PJ drinks in a breath of deep air. "Listen..."

Cyrano is not having it. He jumps over her words with, "No, you hear me first. Look, I don't want to be mean. And I have no need to be cruel to you. But you are certifiable if you think you can convince me that you have no idea why I am upset with you."

PJ pauses, assembles her mental self and draws in a second, deep breath,

"OK, I know that it is difficult for you to believe, but I really do not. And as much as I fear the answer, could you maybe give me a recap?"

Something about the desperation on PJ's face strikes a mercy chord with Cyrano.

And he begins,

"PJ, last Wednesday, you showed up at my house claiming you were lost. You fed me some lame story about looking for a home on the market and then you pretended to recognize me from high school."

PJ, horrified, clings to each syllable that erupts from his perfect lips. Even in her horror, his lips are not lost on her.

He continues, "You also claimed that your cell had no signal, so because I vaguely remembered something about you from school, I offered you the land line.

You followed me into my kitchen, I lifted the receiver and turned to hand it to you. You pounced on me like a starving cougar cramming your tongue down my throat and caressing my crotch. I pushed you away and screamed,

"What the hell do you think you are doing?"

You gave me this wild, maniacal look and said:

"I have gotten your messages. Are you happy I am here? You sent for me!"

I said, "You! Get out! And then it was like the cougar switched off for just a moment. Like someone hit a switch. You looked confused and turned and walked calmly to the door as if nothing had just happened.

You said, "Well, thanks for having me, I guess." And then you left.

Tears are now flowing down both cheeks, a watery reminder of PJ's complete and utter humiliation. She reaches inside her Kate Spade wristlet for a wadded up tissue. Meticulously she opens it and buries her face, sobbing. The most devastating fact of all is her vague discernment convincing her that every word he utters is true.

All the disgust evaporates out of Cyrano. He no longer despises her either.

How can one hate a mentally ill person? And clearly she is a candidate.

PJ excuses herself to the restroom, blows her nose on toilet paper she pulls from the roll on the wall and repairs her wilted face. She studies her reflection in the tiny bathroom mirror.

Time to come clean, Peyton Jane.

She returns to her seat and begins, "I am so immensely sorry and completely humiliated. I cannot conceive nor can I remember doing any of that to you. Please let me try to explain." PJ is pleading now.

"Well, I did come for an answer," Cyrano softly tells her.

"Around a month ago, I was scrolling Facebook and I read your post about the love of your life," PJ confesses. It felt good to confess. Cleanses the palate, so to speak.

"I remember making that post, yeah," Cyrano returns.

"Well, for some reason I got it in my head that you were talking about me. Those cryptic clues about the marriage and the kids and the movies, well, my mind went check, check and check. I know it as ridiculous as Charlie Manson thinking The Beatles were sending him secret messages in their songs, but something stirred in me," PJ explains.

Cyrano is listening intently but saying nothing. His deep, grey eyes are searching her for some sign of deception but even though he is trying to find some, he does not.

PJ resumes, "I am happily married and my husband is an amazing person. I have lived with the shame of my thoughts all these weeks. I went to see a therapist who specializes in hypnosis and I begged him to get

173

you, I mean this, out of my head. It has been consuming me."

"I see." Even he is starting to piece it together.

PJ continues, "Clearly, something has gone terribly wrong if I attacked you and I am mortified beyond my ability to express it. Those things I did to you are the exact opposite of my true desire and I don't even have a clue how to ask you to forgive me for it. And I am also distraught because I have now technically become an adulteress."

Cyrano gives an instant response.

"I think I might believe you. Otherwise, I would have to think you are hands down the most convincing liar I have ever encountered. You seem genuine. If it gives you any peace, I did not write that for you. I did not have the courage to express my love for a very special person back then because I was afraid. PJ, I am gay. I could not tell him then how I felt and now he is married to another man and they have two beautiful sons. I was writing to him."

Instantly, Cyrano and his velvet words evaporate from her heart. She has no doubt now, it isn't even a close race. He is not talking to her. Or about her. Peyton never stood a chance for his affections.

It is this revelation that dissolves the remainder of PJ's all-encompassing obsession for the aesthetic specimen before her. Stunned, she simply says,

"Thank you for telling me that."

"No problem. It was the eighties, Peyton. Homosexuality was still an abomination back then. I had no courage to come out."

"No, I get it." PJ doesn't mention it still is an abomination to her. There is no reason to now, he has just released her from her burden, something Dr. Fisher has failed to do.

"And PJ..."

"Hmmm?"

"I think you need a new doctor."

Jeff Wakes Up

From across the hospital room, Calliope is watching Jeff sleep. He stirs a bit, makes a face and rubs the back of his neck with his left hand. He bolts awake and takes just a moment to adjust his eyes to the light and his brain to consciousness before declaring in his raspy morning voice:

"Well, hello beautiful."

"Lovey dove," she flirts.

"You feeling ok?" Jeff yawns back to his wife.

"I guess. Dr. Abraham is coming soon to give us some new test results," Calliope answers.

"That's good. Have you had breakfast?"

"Not yet but I can hear them delivering it down the hall." Cee Cee informs him.

"Are you ok if I run downstairs and grab something, then?" Jeff gently asks.

"No, babe, go ahead. You need to eat. Get something healthy," she nags.

"Yes, ma'am. Slave driver…." He smiles at her feeble attempt to play wifers.

Calliope blows Jeff a kiss which he catches in the air and rubs hard into his heart. Jeff stands and exits the room and steps down the five flights to the hospital cafeteria.

Upon arriving at the food line Jeff thinks that Cee Cee will be thrilled because there are no other choices beyond healthy. So he settles on a banana, oatmeal and a strawberry yogurt. He pours some thick black coffee and sits down at a table to eat. After finishing his meal, he declares to himself: "I am going to need a big lunch."

Cee Cee is finished with her meal when Jeff returns to her side. He investigates the plate stains and then declares: "Hey! You got biscuits and gravy!"

Calliope answers his exclamation saying: "I know, right? Did anyone tell them what I do for a living?"

"I guess not! That Ford agency might have two cents to put in on this carb fest."

"No kidding." The floor nurse on duty enters the room and approaches the hospital bed.

"Are you finished, sweetie?" she asks as she lifts the empty tray.

"Yup. It was pretty good for hospital fare, too."

The nurse smiles and says, "Glad you liked it. Dr. Abraham is in with the patient next door and then she should be in to talk with you."

"Sounds stellar, thanks." Calliope returns.

The nurse repositions Calliope's tray in her hands and exits the room. Rosie, the housekeeping staff, enters right behind her with her customary mop and begins perfecting the floor. Cee Cee was admitted to this room almost five days prior, and so Jeff has acquired some items which, in this microscopic place, are preventing Rosie from completing her daily tasks.

"Here," Jeff said to Rosie, "let me get that." Jeff rose quickly to his feet to pick up a small suitcase, some flowers and a few shopping bags that are strewn across the tile.

Rosie replies, "It's alright, I'm used to it."

At that, all three laugh and agree the room, although private, is not ample. Rosie continues on as best she can and then mops her way into the bathroom to wipe the fixtures and assess the tub. While she is still cleaning the mirror, the elusive Dr. Abraham enters Calliope's room.

"Good morning, Miss Cash. How are you feeling today?"

Dr. Abraham makes sure her tone is even because she does not like being called Bigfoot and she wants Calliope to know how stupid she thinks her profession is so she intentionally does not appear star struck. Her nurses, however, do not agree and have solicited several autographs each. This enrages the good doctor.

"I'm waiting for you to tell me how I am." Cee Cee is on to the Dr. A game and despises physicians with superiority complexes and no bedside manners.

Smart ass.

"Hmm." The good doctor does not play games. "As you know, we performed a CT scan when you arrived here to assess the swelling in your brain from the fall and an MRI to locate that swelling. Normally, when a person falls over ten feet, there are severe internal complications. Because we cannot be sure just how

178

high you were when you fell, we needed to verify the damage or lack thereof."

Jeff interjects, "What are you saying to us? Is she ok?"

"We can find no damage at this time, no sign of any permanent injury other than the anal tearing and the swelling we did see five days ago was minimal and no longer appearing on any test result," Dr. Abraham finishes up.

Calliope furrows her brow and then says, "Then why was I unconscious and furthermore why did you induce a coma?"

Why, yes, Ms. Smarty Pants. I know some big words as well.

"Allow me to explain. Your fall was less than a thirty-foot descent. It was probably closer to 12 feet. There are many factors that determine the severity of each fall. The first one is how you landed. If you had landed on your feet, you may not even have needed to be seen. If you had landed on your head, we might be fitting you for a wheelchair. Because you landed on your back, your whole body, head and neck absorbed the force of the fall. There was nothing to break your fall. This knocked you unconscious. We simply gave you a drug that left you there until we could assess the extent of your injuries. It was coma like, but not technically a coma and it was for your own good.

Now, if you had gotten ten more feet into the climb, and then fallen, we would be having an entirely different conversation right now. The sudden deceleration and the surface you landed on play into the result as well. Landing on a concrete surface is certainly less preferable as say carpet."

"Or feathers," Cee Cee quips.

Dr. Abraham, unamused, ignores her comment and continues,

"The thing to focus on here is that there is no cerebral edema, no intracranial pressure and really no reason not to discharge you at this time."

Jeff pipes in, "Now we're talkin'."

"I want you to follow up with an OBGYN immediately. There appears to be no damage to the fetus at this time, but we need to get that Bulimia looked at as soon as possible. An embryo needs adequate nutrition and you have missed the first trimester and entered the second with no awareness of that." Abraham is matter of fact here.

Calliope looks ashamed for the first time since entering the hospital. She is beaten because her hidden flaw may just mar someone else, someone totally innocent.

"I will make that appointment today," she replies meekly.

The doctor goes on,

"In addition, I have called downstairs and scheduled a colonoscopy. You will need to do the twenty-four hour prep beforehand."

Calliope sees the satisfaction on her physician's face.

You are a sicko.

"Will there be any risk to the baby?" Cee Cee queries.

"Not if you are careful and follow each instruction to the letter," she offers as she exits through the door.

The unnamed nurse enters the hospital room pushing an ultrasound cart and carrying two belly belts, one blue and one pink. She plugs the baby monitor into the wall and hooks both belts into the unit. Calliope rolls to her left side and allows the nurse to attach both belts, one above her navel and one just below.

"One for a boy and one for a girl," Cee Cee comments.

Because this particular comment is the one this nurse hears more than any other, she simply smiles and continues. Rosie enters as Cee Cee is making a face behind the nurse's back. She returns the expression and Calliope has to place her hand over her mouth to keep from laughing out loud. Rosie likes this patient, she is not demanding and she treats Rosie with respect.

Cee Cee ignores the nurse and what she is doing, she isn't nice anyway, and speaks to Rosie:

"I really do think they gave us the tiniest room on this ward. It is microscopic."

"Yes, child, we call this one "The Closet." It's plum awful and they is prob'ly charging you regular price for this little breath of nothing," Rosie offers.

Cee Cee laughs and tells her, "Well, at least we have good insurance!"

Rosie quips back, "It ain't that old Obamacare, is it?"

"Nah, it's a privately held company," Calliope answers.

"That's good, that's good," Rosie responds as she mops her way back out of Calliope's room.

The Next Morning

Jeff places the last pair of clean pajamas into Calliope's suitcase and listens for the showerhead to quit. He lifts the soft Egyptian cotton towel, the one he brought from home, from the heater vent and goes to his bride. As she exits the shower, he wraps her in the comfort of a good thread count.

"Thanks my love," she gives him. She says it every time because Jeff wraps her each time he is home.

He plants a love tap on her cheek and resumes his packing. He is ready to take his girl home. "I am so glad we are leaving, Cee."

"Me too, Boo Bear." Cee Cee pulls on a shirt and jeans and sits up in the chair by the bed.

"I mean it. I was really scared when I first got here. They made me sign as medical power of attorney on you! I thought you were dying." Jeff looks scared remembering the moment.

"Do I have one for you?" Cee Cee asks.

Jeff informs her, "Apparently, that's what "I Do", did!"

"Cool beans. What's left for me to do?" she asks her groom.

"Just the colonoscopy your other doctor ordered," Jeff replies.

Cee Cee drones, "Well, that sounds like a thrill ride for me."

Jeff laughs at first and then responds, "You know babe, we do need to talk about that at some point. I want to wait until after the procedure to find out if there is any internal damage, but then we have got to try to piece this together. I love you hard enough to forgive just about anything and I understand if you might have found yourself in a tough position with a director or whatever…"

Calliope straightens herself up in the chair and looks her husband square in the eyes.

"I have nothing to tell you. I have no idea how that happened." Calliope is adamant.

"That is good enough for me." He knows he will pursue it later.

An older, experienced nurse enters the room and states:

"Time for your pre-screening, Ms. Cash. I'll get a chair and take you down."

"Ok, thanks. Wait, do you actually thank someone for that?" Jeff and the nurse snicker at her remark.

Jeff says: "If anyone in the outside world had any reasonable clue about how hilarious you are, they would sign you up for stand-up comedy and give you an HBO special."

The nurse agrees with a quick nod.

As Calliope is wheeled toward the elevator, she passes a huge bay window on the North side of the hospital and can't help but notice the Sun parked low in the morning sky.

Others are having coffee and I am making arrangements to be legally violated.

The nurse wheels her patient into the outer corridor where all proctology patients are seen.

A male medical resident, caught up in his own accomplishments, hands Calliope a clipboard with a questionnaire. She carefully answers the questions and hands it back to the staff.

Cee Cee is taken into a small, sterile office where she waits to be seen. A strapping and handsome young intern, a different one, enters the room and takes a seat across from her.

How does anyone in their right mind PICK proctology? I mean, how does one start studying anatomy and then suddenly, all at once, get the revelation: Hey, I think I would really like to look up butts?

This opinion is solely based on what comes out of them.

Back to Romeo, the Intern

Romeo says: "So, this is a pre-screening?"

Cee Cee answers, "Mmm, hmm. But I think they want to do it as soon as possible. I missed an appointment for this last year."

"OK, well do you have any concerns? Other than the prep?" Romeo is nothing if not thorough.

"Nope. It sounds so fun!" Cee Cee tells him dripping sarcasm.

Romeo begins tapping madly on a lap top. This goes on long enough for Calliope to wonder just how long it takes to type: Nope.

The real doctor enters, sits beside Cee Cee and says: "How's it going?"

"Good, but deja woo, huh?" she smiles at her doctor. She likes him, he plays her game.

The doctor replies, "Yeah, didn't we have you scheduled in late November? As I recall, you have a family history of colon issues and we were just checking, right? Are you ready for this?"

Calliope lowers her head and peers over imaginary glasses as she states, "Is anyone ever ready for this?"

Laughing, he returns, "I guess not. Stop outside at the desk for a procedure time."

"OK, I guess I will see you later since you stood me up the week of Thanksgiving."

He laughs.

"You know," she continues,

"I could not believe that you would have rather been having dinner with your family instead of performing my colonoscopy. Cannot understand how you had better things to do."

The doctor loves this game. "Yeah, it's a mystery!"

Now it is her turn to laugh.

Calliope is wheeled once again down a corridor and positioned in front of a desk. Sarah of surgery asks: "So, what are we scheduling today young lady?"

Matter of factly, Cee Cee replies, "Well, Dr. D down there wants to cram a camera up my rear end."

Sarah of Surgery replies, "Ooooohhhhh kkkkkaaaayyyy....."

"Oh, come on, don't tell me you haven't heard it all by now," Calliope offers up.

"Oh, believe me I have, and still that is a unique declaration."

"Well, just schedule it for me please because if you don't put something on paper today it won't get done and I won't call back. I don't know anyone who would." She is just stating facts.

"Oh, it will happen day after tomorrow, let's pencil in 10:00 am."

Sarah of Surgery marks it down in her book.

"It's a date!" Calliope exclaims.

As Cee Cee is being taken out of the exam area, she is stopped by two women at a reception desk.

The pruney faced older woman on the right inquires: "What doctor did you see today?"

"Dr. D. I mean Denning, Dr. Denning." Pruney face scowls. This is as good as a challenge for Calliope. It is like prune face threw down the gauntlet. She must laugh or die.

"Do you need to come back?" Pruney plods on.

"Oh, yes, Dr. D wants to put an apparatus up my tailpipe." Lady on the left is dying. Prune face-no reaction.

Calliope, relentless, continues," You know, we are having a big celebration in honor of the procedure and you are invited. We are serving collard greens, prunes and broccoli. Bring the family!"

The lady on the left is wiping away tears. Prune face-nothin'.

"WOW." Calliope states. "Tough crowd."

REVELATIONS

Vinnie Bleeds Out

"Boss, I didn't think I would have to beg youse for my life tonight. I gots no idea what that is. I do not recall it, maybe I blacked out or something. That is so weird to watch the video because I don't even know where that room is."

I guess this is it. I expected it to eventually happen, but I thought I might have some idea why. At least I won't have to watch the rearview any longer.

"Vinnie, you expect me to believe you don't know where you were when you were standing right there. Come on, you need to tell me what happened." Boss is starting to get annoyed.

The ogre behind Vinnie whacks him in the back of the head with a large socket wrench. Vinnie grunts and bleeds but that is all. The muscleman rolls and repositions the wrench in his hand, the literal tool of his trade. He is preparing for strike two.

"Boss, you can beat me blue but I gots no idea. I have been seeing a doctor for my little episodes and I have had a few blackouts that I was scared to tell you about but I gots no idea why I am on that disc."

"Where is my money, Vinnie?" Boss wants to believe him, he even sort of does believe him, but the footage screams something else.

"I don't know." Another blow from the wrench. The blood is running in rivers down both sides of his head now.

"Vinnie, you been a good employee but I need some answers. You is making me look like a chump here and this is not a fuggettaboutit." Boss begins to raise his voice and screech Vinnie's Christian name:

"VINCENT, VINCENT, VINCENT......"

Vinnie's eyes gloss over and his countenance alters. His speech and movement become unresponsive and robotic, a condition not lost on the witnesses.

"Where are we?" Vinnie asks the guys. "What's with the plastic? Am I on the job?" The two other men turn and stare at their captive.

"Vinnie. Vinnie! What the hell is wrong wid you?" Nicky screams.

Vinnie does not respond and instead takes on a catatonic appearance.

"I'm not playing wid you," he continues.

Carmine is the first person to make the connection.

"Boss. Look. He is same in the video. He is acting like some freakin' zombie. Like somebody is programming him to do this shit."

Vinnie continues, "This plastic is so crackly. Geez, I have a head ache."

"Didn't he say he has been seeing some hypnotist doctor?" Boss barks.

Vinnie shuffles his feet on the plastic and announces, "Hey, guys, listen to this!" The plastic whinnies under Vinnie's dress shoes. Vinnie laughs and says, "It sounds like I'm skiing!"

"Yea, we picked him up from the medical building," Nicky answers.

Vinnie's boss once again looks at the video that much earlier put his stomach in knots. He too notices the inconsistency in Vinnie's personality.

"This makes me want some warm cappuccino," Vinnie continues to babble.

"VINCENT CARMINE CASTANA, snap out of it!" At the sound of his full Christian name, Vinnie does just that.

Tropical Storm Jeff

Jeff and Calliope are finally home. It is the later Jeff was talking about at the hospital. They have begun the war that is bubbling just beneath the surface.

"Honey! I am NOT accusing you! Please listen to me," Jeff pleads.

"Well it sure as hell sounds like you are accusing me of something…"

Jeff takes a deep breath, lowers his head, and slowly states,

"Calliope Grace. I love you dearly with every breath in me. But someone has done damage to you and we both know it was not me."

"Jeff, you know I don't let people do that to me. If I won't let you, no one else stands a chance either," Cee Cee answers him. She is desperate for his support and belief.

"Is there any possibility you could have been drugged or had too much to drink on a job?" Jeff is reaching. Cee Cee runs her hand through her hair exasperated by the length of this interrogation.

Calliope replies,

"Husband. Love of my life. I cannot think of even one moment I was not completely and utterly coherent. There is no one in my life who has that much access to me unless I was completely out of my mind or hypnotized or some…"

Fear and realization cross her face simultaneously and she cannot complete the word much less the sentence.

Jeff looks at her with the same thoughts running through his mind and at the same speed. He speaks first,

"Oh, shit."

Calliope's Dream

His legs are dangling.   There is no life. It's a puppet
on his master's lap. The morbid grin of Mortimer
Snerd turning slowly, slowly to face Calliope. He
winks at her.

"My pretty, my pretty......" and then Mortimer's face
becomes histrionic and wicked morphing into Dr.
Fisher's face, and then Calliope's.

Cee Cee presses down hard on her eyelids and
allows the light to wake her. She closes them again,
fluttering against the fireworks forming under the lids.
Neon flowers blooming and dissipating, erupting and
dissolving as she fights back against the day, trying to
keep them closed while bright white clouds eat away
at the dark.

I'm up.

But she isn't really up. She is only half conscious, in
the midst of that point each morning where the mind
is clearer and thoughts are much easier to sort. She
begins to analyze her own dream, knowing now that
she indeed, is a puppet. An unwilling vessel just
reacting to the strings Dr. Fisher pulls. It is a true
breath of total terror to not know what she has done
or even what has been done. It is almost a greater
violation than The Incident because she is unaware of
when and how she has been raped. Or how many
times. Or where. The anal tearing is one clue, but it is
only one effect of a seven-month violation of her
psyche and her flesh. It is a prolonged battery, a
relentless, unpermitted touching.

Instantly, ten separate memories fight for pole position in her mind. She can see herself walking into the medical complex in a Michael Kors skirt and then a rewind and it is a Tommy Hilfiger dress and then rewind again with another outfit, another season.

The weather changed! Oh my God! I HAVE been there more than twice! Oh, God! He IS raping me while I am under hypnosis! Why can I not remember it clearly?

In one sense, she is grateful to have no memory of one specific rape. It is a disgusting way to have a woman as your own. But she simply can't shake the thought that it leaves too much room for speculation as to what else has occurred. Her thoughts are eating her alive.

Time to baptize another pillow.

Further Revelation

Calliope sits confused and scared. A mass of memories, or what she perceives as real memories stir in her head. She finishes her crying, she cannot produce any more water than she already has.

This isn't making sense? How can this be? I distinctly remember that first session. Jeff and I ate at Fab Patty's right after the appointment. He asked me how my first session went? Didn't he? Wait! Jeff made that face, that what the crap are you talking about face? He said first, or at least I think that he did. Did he? What am I really remembering and what am I being programmed to remember? And how in heaven will I ever prove any of this? What did Jeff say when he asked about the session and I told him Dr. Fisher seemed nice? Was it "Hmmm"?

Calliope's memory is racing. She knows that she remembers Jeff's surprised expression.

He DID make a face. Didn't HE? Am I going crazy here? Why didn't he ask me what he was thinking? I remember...I remember...what the heck do I remember? I don't even know.

Calliope closes her eyes hard and tries to calm her racing thoughts. Every image is lining up and sitting like sentences in her mind. Every thought racing, evenly aligned like the words of a story building to some grandiose point. But this is different. This is blank. There are bubbles surfacing and then popping before the full image blows up. Things are vaguely familiar and then nothing. Immediately she returns to a tan leather couch and she is being bent over it with her face succumbing to the adhesiveness of the hide.

I remember thinking that I might leave a cheek print in this grain. I can hear grunting and panting and someone saying: "Oh, dear gawd this girl is tight!" My mind won't register it- it's protecting me like it did on a cold floor ten years ago. I cannot stay here, I will combust.

Then Calliope hears her own voice in memory.

"Wrong hole, you jerk!" Strangely, I did not scream. Why didn't I scream?! Is this what actually happened? No! No! NO! Not my body again! Did I? Did he?

She has held it in as long as she can and so she buries her face into the feather pillow and baptizes it properly for the second time this morning.

Calliope promised the universe after the Incident that no one else would ever touch her until the one man she loves did. And she kept that covenant until her wedding night. No premarital maneuvers, none whatsoever.

Calliope hides the assault, holds it closely to herself, strong enough, she thinks, to provide her own therapy. She does not house the usual guilt of a victim. She puts things in the proper perspective. Those guys were animals. What they did to her was feral and criminal. Calliope protects this memory for one reason alone. She doesn't want it to hold any power over her. She will not let it ruin her. Not many girls can do that. And every now and then, just like

her last meal, it creeps back in and takes up a
temporary residence.

The Incident, Revisited

Just after her attackers retreated, Calliope gathered her broken self, wiped away the things that could be removed with paper bathroom towels and stumbled toward the riverbank. She slowly lowered herself to the warm grass. Calliope remembers most vividly the waves. Specifically, the way the river crocheted a path across to the other side of the bank snaking back and forth. She was struck by the proximity of such ugliness and such astounding beauty. The rape and the river occurred within yards of the other. It was at that moment she determined her future-to be the ultimate, most stunning and most importantly, untouchable image of woman. She would give them but a glimpse, a page, but no man will ever do that to me again. The rape challenged her to rise above it. It beckoned her to rise above. And that is exactly what she did.

 The closest any man will ever get to me again is to turn the page.

It would have been so easy to catch my attackers. I had a timeline, a utility truck and a detailed description of each one of those three monsters. No one will ever understand why I could not do that. Not even if you were a woman who had experienced something similar, most victims do just the opposite- they camouflage their beauty, their desirability even by gaining weight in excessive amounts, layering themselves for protection. Buffering themselves. Suppressing it wasn't what I wanted, it was my only option.

How could I have gone home and explained that to my mother? What would her eyes have held for me after that? And Ann, my sister? Some sick side of her might have been satiated by the damage to her perfect sibling. Ah, yes, the obedient one gets her "due". She may have been thrilled when I finally had my terrible, horrible, no-good, very bad day.

I had no choice but to gather what was left of me and call home. It was the first time I had ever lied to my mother.

I remember walking to my Jeep, still unlocked, with the keys in the ignition. I turned on the motor, blasted the air conditioner. My Coach bag sat sentinel in the passenger seat undisturbed. I reached deep within the contents and retrieved my cell phone, a Motorola Razor. With bloodied skinned-up fingers, I dialed home trying to suppress the memory of how I obtained those wounds.

Mom picked up on the second ring. She always did that as if she wanted you to know that she definitely was interested in taking your call but she would give you two rings to make sure you wanted to ring her in the first place.

"Hello?" Mom answered.

"Mom."

"Hey, C. How'd the shoot go?"

"Aw, it was good, but I left early." I told her.

"Why for?" she asked me.

"Camera jam." Not a lie.

"I prefer grape. Ha,ha,ha. Is you is?" she said.

I loved it when she said it that way. My mother, the English Queen, who could write a paragraph that would make Hemingway jealous, never said: "Where are you?" It was always: "Is you is?"

"I'm at the coffee shop." (*First lie.*)" I just need to unwind a bit." (*Second lie. I needed to scream*). "Rachel wants me to crash with her for a few days-are you good with that?" (*And that folks, was number three.*)

"Did you girls check with the parental unit?" Mom went on.

"She is on board." I told her.

"OK. Bon voyage, sister!" She sent me off.

"Mom..."

"Hmmm?"

"I love you." I meant it.

"Back at ya', lovey dove." She meant it, too.

"I will call you tomorrow, ok?" (Not a lie.)

"Ok, sis. Be safe. Make good decisions!" she instructed.

"I will."

But I did not go to Rachel instead I called for a reservation. Saving all my babysitting cash and the funds from local modeling gigs provided me with the income to secure the privacy I desperately needed. I put the Jeep in gear ignoring the screaming transmission and drove quickly to a local hotel. I checked in to The Very Thing and dropped on the bed.

In movies, you always see rape victims heading directly to a shower to wash off the attack. By this time, I had held in too much, too long. Burying my face into a cheap polyester pillow, I drenched the 200 count cover. This went on for a while. I wept and I slept. When I awakened for good, I staggered toward the bathroom and took the proverbial shower, no longer or shorter than my usual ritual. Removing a sandpaper towel from the chrome rack, I placed it carefully over the mirror to obscure my view. I couldn't handle seeing the violated version of me. Maybe if I had known then that my mother had an expiration date-that I only had months left to love her-maybe then I would have confessed it all, crying and heaving and hugging the life out of her. She could have wept it out for me and like any mother, made it better. God, how I miss that woman. No one should ever lose a parent in the twisted metal of a texting teen. Not ever. It's ironic and unfair. She never even carried a cell phone. She certainly did not deserve to die at the hand of one. Or because some stupid kid had one velcroed to her hand.

Then the realization hits her like an unexpected slap.

Someone HAS done it to me again. Despite my independent mental health, plan someone penetrated my safe zone. My security. And the saddest fact is, I basically gave my permission when I allowed him into my brain. What the hell was I thinking?

And why does this keep happening to me?

PJ Unloaded

PJ needs to talk. She has to unload all that has happened and she can't tell Brad. It is her fault she is in this mess and she needs to fix it. But if she does not tell someone, she is going to combust. Spontaneously. Big firey mess.

Peyton opens up her Iphone and scrolls down for Sharon's number. She dials it and Sharon picks up on the second ring. After giving her a brief description of her distress, she begs her to come see her as soon as she can and so Sharon is en route. Because Sharon is a great friend. Peyton is waiting for her now.

How much will I tell her? I know I can trust her if for no other reason than all the crap I have on her. I would never ever use it, though. She is like blood to me. I need to bounce some of this off of someone and maybe they can help me sort it out. And figure it out. And then make that bastard pay......

The front doorbell rings, Sharon opens the door and yells, "Yoo hoo!"

"In here," Peyton yells back.

"Hey girl. How they hanging?" Sharon is a riot.

"Ha, ha, ha. Sit down 'cause today I need a good listening ear. And a friend. That is why I called you."

"What's up? Kids, ok? Brad?" she asks.

"Oh, yeah, they are awesome. I, however, am about to blow a gasket," Peyton tells her.

"Whew! Sounds juicy. Let me grab a green tea and settle in," Sharon answers.

Sharon works her way to the refrigerator and grabs a bottle of diet green tea with berry, opens a drawer and snags the rubber jar opener and begins turning the top on the bottle.

"Damn thing is always on too tight," she dictates to herself. She returns to the great room where PJ is sitting and joins her on the Broyhill couch.

"Let me have it," she informs her friend.

PJ takes a deep breath and begins: "I don't know where to start..."

Hurricane Jeff

"He raped you, babe. Over and over. He needs to go to jail and experience that for himself," Jeff pleads with his wife.

"Sit down, husband." Calliope is commanding him now. Jeff does as he is told.

"It has happened before...."
"When? What are you??? On the Hypothesis campaign? When? What are you telling me?" Jeff is frantically questioning his wife.

"Babe, just listen to me. I was only fifteen and I had gone into town to work up some shots for my portfolio. A man abducted me and took me to a deserted park restroom. He and two other guys assaulted me. I never told anyone that. I didn't want anyone to know what had happened to me and I thought I could handle it on my own," Cee Cee cries softly as she continues to explain.

Jeff, his breath taken away, can only sit and listen to the details. Then he cries with her. Jeff speaks first:

"I am destroyed that any man treated you that way. My princess. But this crazy doctor has been using you for almost nine months now and we have to put a stop to it." Jeff is desperate for justice.

"Jeff, I am not going back!" Cee Cee is insistent.
"That is not what I mean, honey. He will do this again. We have to do something to keep it from happening to anyone else. It is the only right way to go."

Jeff tries to reason with his wife but she is blinded by her embarrassment.

Calliope pleads, "I can't. I just can't. It was so hard the first time. And I don't even know for sure what he has done."

The sentence Jeff stated before finally resonates in her mind.

"Wait! What did you just say? Nine months?! Jeff, are you telling me that I really HAVE been in therapy for almost nine months?"

For whatever reason, Cee Cee is playing dumb, trying to resurrect Jeff's memory before she can trust her own. She has no recognizable timeline in her own twisted memory so she must rely on Jeff's knowledge now.

"Yeah, babe. Almost nine," he tells her.

"I can't even get my brain out of park. How can it be that I do not remember any of this? I thought I had only been there twice. I have no trouble remembering the initial visit, it was brief and then later he asked me questions to see if I would be a good candidate for hypnosis. That is all I can draw up. All I can recall," Cee Cee responds.

"Babe," Jeff continues, "you started back in March near the first part of the month."

"And if I am sixteen weeks now, then you got me pregnant around mid-July. At least, I hope YOU did."

"Oh, my God, Cee Cee, I cannot even conceive of anything else right now," Jeff wimpers.

"Honey, we have to consider it a possibility." It is killing Calliope to say that sentence.

Jeff, weakened by the notion, responds forcefully: "I will not. Not ever. That child is MINE. This much I know."

Cee Cee smiles at her husband. "Good answer. Now how do we prove any of this?"

Until this exchange, Jeff had not stopped to consider his unborn child. So he sits, quietly rethinking his position. He has just made his first verbal claim to his offspring and experienced an instantaneous shift of priorities.

Jeff answers his exasperated wife, "Well, now I am not so sure that we can or even if we should. Can you imagine the publicity? We want to be anonymous. It will never happen if something like this gets out. They will never leave us alone."

"I know you are right but I cannot stand the thought of that man..." she trails off. "Hypothesis will cancel my campaign and I will be tarnished goods. I know they will. They won't want their brand connected to this sordid affair."

"And we have someone else to consider now," Jeff acknowledges.

Rubbing her belly lovingly, "Jeff, I have already denied him too much. There is no need to add the stress of a trial. I want to fully commit to this child, our child. I am in awe of how happy he has made me."

"Or she!"

Piper Arrington

Calliope crosses the room of the home they share
and kisses her husband deeply.

PJ Buddies Up

"OK," Sharon answers, "let me see if I get this. You went to see a therapist hoping he would take a guy out of your head so you could get on with your life with Brad and the kids. Instead, he sends you over to the guy's house and makes you jump his bones."

PJ sensing the underlying sarcasm smirks when she confirms, "That is exactly what happened. I know it is unbelievable."

"So let me ask you this. For what reason would he do that? It's so stupid!"

Sharon trusts her friend, but their relationship is such that she can question the validity of her story without affecting the relationship between them.

"That I do not know. It is a really sick thing to pull off. But I am scared because I don't know what else he might have made me do if I have no recollection of this ridiculous mess!" PJ defensively replies.

Sharon studies her friend's expression for a moment and decides that at the minimum, PJ believes it has happened. She is not completely sold on the idea that Dr. Fisher has done anything but maybe messed up her good friend's head a bit. She has no doubt that PJ is not lying, but it doesn't necessarily mean the story is true either. It's a lot to swallow.

"PJ, I do not know how to help you. But maybe we can talk it through some more and devise a plan of action to confirm what you think happened.

"It did happen, Sharon! Cyrano told me!" PJ is desperate for her friend's support.

"Look, if he did this, he needs to be in jail. You can't just destroy a family especially when his patient is trying to save it. He needs to lose his license or something if we can prove he did this. And if we cannot prove it but we know he did it, we will write him a prescription for payback. I just don't know what that means yet."

Vinnie in Another Room

Vinnie is home. Boss, not really wanting to eliminate Vincent in the first place, releases him after witnessing his confusion. Vinnie is not clear how or why he ended up on that video tape, but he is bound to find out. There is no one thing that screams hypnotism, but he knows deep down there is something very fishy about the good doc Fisher.

I will get him. In due time, I will get him for sure.

Vinnie is watching *The Vikings*. This he considers job training. He admires the machismo of these primeval warriors and their prowess in annihilating the human body. Vinnie studies the evil people of history.

Vinnie likes the Mayans as well. He is mesmerized by their affinity to rip a beating heart from the body. It is a unique way to sign an execution. Vinnie puts his signature on every kill as well, by never using the same method twice. This is his signature, true versatility. The only running theme is dependent on his relationship with the assignment. If Vinnie is asked to "off" a friend, he is more merciful. A bullet to the skull. A wire around the neck. Despite having no conscience, he does value friendship enough to at least make any parting swift. On the other hand, a rat needs to suffer. The death of a rat is a teaching tool for the others.

So Vinnie does his homework. If he had ever learned how to actually use a bow, he would have delighted in exploding someone's head with numerous arrows in the same manner as his heroes, the Vikings. He finds the exploding brain unique and creative. One of those

214

ideas he wishes had been his own. Although he figures it is probably a bit messy. You have to consider the cleanup.

He is currently a student of The Blood Eagle, another offering of the Vikings. He wants to use it on his next rat job but he has not quite worked out how to pull it off. It involves an extremely precise series of incisions to the back rib section followed by a technique of breaking the rib bones and turning them up to resemble angel wings. The lungs are then pulled through the incisions and left outside the body, still attached.

Vinnie says out loud to himself: "Youse talk, youse don't breathe. Rest with the angels."

Considering his occupation as a hit man, he is inordinately poetic. Vincent Castana, mesmerized by the gore before him, plans his next rat hunt.

PJ Storming

Peyton Jane quickens her pace as she crosses the intersection. She steps onto the curb, hugs the building and bears right. As she enters the medical complex housing Dr. Fisher's office, she preps herself for battle. She is feeling both angry and powerful as she chooses the stairs and leaps them two at a time.

Peyton arrives at the third floor barely winded, adrenaline supplying her needs as she pushes open the exit door and makes the left turn to her therapist's office.

Miss Honeycut barely attends to PJ as she storms in. PJ does not acknowledge the curt receptionist choosing to bypass her desk and throw open Steven's office door. Miss Honeycut immediately intervenes when she stands up, saying:

 "Excuse me but you may not go in unannounced."

"Can it, whinese," Peyton returns satisfied to finally let her know what she sounds like. Miss Honeycut looks like a injured animal as she has never been treated so harshly by a patient and all she can do is to lower herself back into her chair and nurse her wounds. PJ continues in to the doctor's lair.

"I KNOW WHAT YOU DID, YOU PIECE OF SHIT!" Peyton screams at Dr. Fisher.

Steven looks up from his notepad and quietly asks her,

"Do you have an appointment?"

PJ's heart is racing and her voice is beginning to tremble.

"Yes, I do! To RUIN you. How dare you play with my life this way! I will go to the media and tell them what you did."

Steven, unshaken as if he knows an escape route Peyton has not figured on, is cool. He is too cool. He seems completely unaffected by her accusation, her tone of voice or threat.

He calmly responds, "No, you won't Peyton. Sit down."
"I am not doing what you say. You cannot exert your control over me anymore. I WILL tell everyone about you. You cannot get away with this. It is wrong on every level. You're a monster, you are!" Peyton is trembling with anger.

"Ah, Peyton. You will not tell anyone. You cannot risk anyone knowing that you are not what they think you are. You are an adulteress. A Sunday School teacher. A hypocrite to the tenth degree. And you cannot stand yourself. You are familiar enough with the Bible to know that the sinning is in the thought of sinning. You walked into this office an adulteress."

 Steven never even looks up at Peyton.

"How dare you say that to me! YOU SENT ME TO THAT MAN'S HOME!"

"I did no such thing. I have no idea to what you are referring."

Steven is still calm and clearly unaffected by her knowledge of his crime. Peyton is emphatic with her reply.

"Yes, you do. Oh, you play it so cool, don't you Dr. Fisher? I see your black heart. You are pure evil and you cannot fix evil. It runs too deep. I am going to expose you for the charlatan you are. People are not puppets for your bidding," PJ explodes.

She is not letting the bad guy win this time.

"You are an innately disturbed woman." Steven remains calm, unflinching. Steven begins to mock her, "Oh, you poor pitiful pious Christian. Everyone who is not like you is evil. Chew on this Sister Christian. Your subconscious mind will perform for you those tasks you are too reserved in the flesh to do. You did not or even could not do anything you were not planning to do. You wanted it, Peyton. That is what you need to know."

PJ is now screaming: "WHAT I THOUGHT I WANTED! I came to you for help. You agreed to help me get him out of my mind not in my pants. I may not be able to connect all the dots yet, but I will and you will answer for what you did."

Then Steven did what Steven does best. He begins to lie. He concocts a tale like a satin-tongued devil with silky smooth syllables, one sliding against the next as if skiing out of his mouth.

"Peyton, I did not want to tell you this before because I know it will cause you great pain, but some interesting things occurred during your sessions and while you were under hypnosis. You made several attempts to seduce me while I was instructing you. Your mind is a powerful organ and you clearly have an iron will and a tendency toward this behavior. This is not an exact Science. If you are dissatisfied with your therapy then…"

PJ did not allow him to finish that sentence interrupting with, "Are you for real right now? There is a huge difference in being dissatisfied with my therapy and knowing that you have manipulated me into an affair. I came here for help and you violated my trust."

Steven studies her face for a moment and then ends their conversation with this statement:

"Perhaps you will consider this a violation as well. I taped it. I taped it all, every session. I have audio of you telling me how you lusted after another man even to the point of imagining him entering you. Does Brad have a CD player in his car? I bet he would be very interested what his wife thinks about…"

"DON'T YOU GO NEAR MY HUSBAND!!!"

"Don't you make me."

PJ Clueless

The phone is ringing. PJ crosses the great room, picks up the receiver and speaks into it.

"Hello?"

"Well?" Sharon queries from the other end of the connection.

"Well, what?" PJ plays back.

"Seriously, PJ? I have to beg for it? What happened with Dr. Fisher?"

PJ confused, responds: "Huh? What are you talking about?"

Sharon also confused, responds in kind, "PJ! You called me on your way to his office. Did you confront him or not?"

"About what, Sharon?" PJ has no idea what her friend is asking her right now.

Sharon, now concerned about her best friend asks, "Are you feeling ok?"

"Yea, I am fine. How are you because you seem to be confused?"

Sharon makes one final effort.

"PJ. Did you go to Dr. Fisher's office today?" Sharon pleads.

"Not that I can recall."

Sharon Shows Up

Sharon is driving faster than her normal speed. Her concern for PJ is a little off the chart. Sharon is actually wondering if her friend is sane. After all, she is seeing a therapist.

Did she lie the first time or did she lie the second? I have never known her to lie so why am I so quick to accuse her even if it's only in my head?

Sharon continues down Route 190 to the large and luxurious subdivision where PJ and Brad reside. She turns first down Nedra Lane, left on Daughtery Circle and then right on Dickson. She puts the car in park and hurries to the door. She rings the bell.

PJ answers as if she is just passing by as it rang.

"Hi, girl. What are you doing here?" PJ queries her.

"We need to talk. I know you are probably traumatized because I know how you feel about confrontations, but you need me and we are going to talk about what you did today."

Sharon wants answers and she is not leaving without them.

"Sister, you tell me and then I will tell you," PJ answers.

"So, you are sticking to the I don't remember line, huh?"

"I DON'T remember!"

Sharon pushes past her friend and heads to the couch in the great room. She plops herself down and then begins,

"Let me refresh your memory for you. You called me to come over and then you told me a story about being enamored of some guy from high school. Then you read an article about Dr. Fisher and you went to see him to have him deprogram this man from your mind because you felt so guilty about it. I checked my phone, PJ. When you texted me, the location device showed you outside that medical complex, so you need to spill your guts. You cannot just tell me that and not tell me how you ended it." Sharon is desperate for information right now. And deeply concerned for her best friend.

PJ is scared and she looks it. Deep in the recesses of her heart, she knows that Sharon is telling the truth but PJ cannot not draw up a clear enough memory to confirm what she is saying.

"Sharon, I don't know what to say. This is frightening for me because I remembered slivers while you were talking. I guess it maybe was not such a great idea to go back there."

"Ya' think?" Sharon does nothing to disguise her sarcasm this time.

"Now, now. Cut me some slack. I am suffering here from amnesia." PJ is continuing the defensive and clueless theme.

"PJ, did he hypnotize you today?" Sharon continues.

"How should I know? He has the perfect method of getting what he wants because I just can't remember what happens. I can't put it all together in my head. It feels more like a dream to me." PJ is confused and defeated.

Sharon is adamant with her last sentence to her friend,

"PJ, he is dangerous. Promise me you won't go back there. Promise me."

PJ answers Sharon,

"I guess I don't really see the point. If I can't even remember going then I am not making much progress, am I?"

Jeff Goes All Forensic Files

Jeff Seaton is on a mission covert enough to keep from his wife. Calliope, now glowing and seven months with his child, is shopping for nursery furniture. She has taken a hiatus from her modeling career in order to focus all her attention on the pregnancy and has not thrown up a meal in twelve weeks. The baby, a boy, is developing on schedule and does not seem to be affected by the trauma his mother endured or the bulimia she suffered with for the first trimester. It is amazing how just the knowledge that a life is dependent on you can cure an eating disorder. It's not been easy but she is so content with the thought of being a family that she has simply willed herself to better health.

Jeff and Cee Cee have decided to put the good doctor behind them. They don't have any clue what Steven has done to Calliope and neither one wants to be so exposed to the public condemnation with this new little fella growing into their lives. So they make the decision for him, still unnamed, to move on. But Jeff just can't do it. Lately he is consumed by the thought that Little Man is not his. He doesn't think he can raise the evil spawn of Dr. Sicko and he wants the answers. He will not tell Calliope any of this but he has taken to stalking the good doctor for three days now. He can't seem to stop himself from thinking there may be a bad seed growing in his beautiful wife. He HAS to know.

Dr. Fisher is not difficult to tail because he follows a specific regimen. At any moment, he will emerge from the health club throwing back a Fiji water. Jeff has seen enough *Forensic Files* to know how to handle throw away DNA. So moments later when Dr. Fisher does indeed emerge and finishes the last half of his water, Jeff slips on a pair of latex gloves, retrieves the bottle from the waste can and places it in a zip locked bag.   He returns to his car and examines the contents rolling it back and forth in his hands.

Baby, Baby

Calliope enters her apartment giddy and refreshed. She calls out to her husband,

"Jeff! Are you home?"

"In here, babe," he answers from the bedroom.

Calliope skips down the hall with a catalog from a local store specializing in baby supplies.

"Wait until you see what I ordered for our little man!"

 She opens the catalog to a dog-eared page and lays it before her groom on their bed. It is marked by the image of a crib that is designed to look like a space ship. The bed is round with an attached canopy shaped liked a NASA rocket. The bedding itself is red, white and blue with the NASA logo strategically located around the exterior.

"Look, the mobile is a mini-universe with all the planets in different colors. They even rotate around the Sun according to the speed of their actual revolutions. Or some similarity to it! Don't you just love it??" Cee Cee excitedly asks him.

"That is about the coolest thing I have ever seen." Though distracted by his day, he means every word.

"Oh, Jeff, I am so pumped. I cannot wait to lay our little boy down in that rocket ship. We might have to name him Astro or something stellar like that."

She is completely serious.

"No son of mine will be named after a dog off *The Jetsons*, Ceece." Jeff kisses her on the cheek. "I love how enthusiastic you are for him."

"Oh, my gosh, I cannot wait to meet him. I hope he looks just like you and sings just like me. Or vice versa!"

"Well, he probably will until he hits puberty...." Jeff teases her.

"Oh, stop. I am serious. He is already the greatest thing I have ever done. When he moves in me I just feel so blessed. I know we did not plan to start this early, but when I think about the doctor saying the fetus is viable, the very first thing I remember feeling was that this must be what Abraham thought when God promised him generations. I mean do you get it? WE ARE GOING ON! There will be more of us! It blows my mind every time I consider it."

Jeff does not speak because he cannot speak. He lifts his wife's chin with his hand and tenderly kisses her mouth.

When he pulls away, she asks him, "What was that for?"

"Because YOU are the greatest thing I have ever done..."

Calliope smiles back at her spouse and waddles down the hallway to the kitchen. Jeff listens as she moves pans about and prepares his dinner. When he is certain she has busied herself, he goes to his duffle bag in the bottom of the bedroom closet. He removes

the Fiji water bottle, frees it from its plastic home and
tosses it in the trash.

The Feast of Eight Fishes

Christmas Eve

Vinnie and Analisa, because they are childless, travel every Christmas Eve to the Jersey shore to help Analisa's three sisters fix The Feast of Seven Fishes. It is a most Catholic tradition. Analisa, Alexa, Ana Maria and Sophia (named after her maternal grandmother) will spend most of this day preparing seven separate fish dishes to honor the seven sacraments and the seven virtues. All the girls have done this since childhood, from the time they could barely peek over the counter.

Analisa tilts her head against the frosty side window of the Cadillac and scans each little town as they drive through light snow to the home of Ana Maria and her betrothed, Nicholas. Analisa loves to window shop the tiny coves and she thinks the snow makes each little annex look like dollhouse villages painted on Currier and Ives Christmas cards. As the Cadillac cruises through Jersey, she studies the high rises, newly constructed, with old patriachs and matriarchs placed just so like index cards in an outdated card catalog. She despises the way these little towns organize the old people into one area as if letting them out would be bad for society. And she worries that she may be one of them someday. She knows more about her husband's job than she ever lets on. Analisa is well aware that the younger generation has not discovered the value of their elders.

Vinnie has not told his betrothed of the bidness he needs to handle later in this evening. He fears

Analisa's disappointed look more than the wrath of the boss and he knows she will be disappointed when he leaves her this Christmas Eve. It could not be helped, he has to take care of that doctor once and forever. He already made the arrangements and the pickup should be occurring right about now. But for now, that is just bidness, and bidness holds no currency on Christmas Eve.

The Caddy is sitting in the driveway of her sister and Analisa steps carefully out of the older vehicle bracing herself against the door. Nicholas salted the sidewalk earlier but Analisa does not trust the mileage on her knees even on a clear path.

Vinnie approaches his bride, offers up an arm and they coast toward the door both walking and sliding in spots. Ana Maria swings open the door dramatically and screams: "Mi famiglia!"

 Then she quickly plants a kiss on four cheeks. After entering the modest home and receiving thirty-two more kisses, Analisa settles herself in the kitchen with the girls. Vinnie moves toward the sound of a televised hockey game.

Ana Maria and the other girls are a cacophony of greetings and simultaneous demands.

"Analisa, you make-a the baccala. No one can make-a like you," Alexa tells her.

Sophia protests immediately,

"I want to make-a the baccala! It's-a my favorite! Analisa can do the puttanesca, no one ever eats the puttanesca when I fix it and it is-a her best dish."

Time for Analisa to set everyone straight. "I no have-a specialty. I can-a make anything you-a want. Anything with-a tomatoes." And with that statement, Analisa purses her bottom lip and nods her head once as if she were saying:

"So there!"

The kitchen erupts with laughter and estrogen as they tease their boastful sibling. Five proud Italian Catholic women prepare seven fish dishes. No red meat will be served this evening in remembrance of Lent.

The table is festively set in red and gold with candles and huge clear bowls of Christmas bulbs. Each chair has been wrapped like a present in alternating gold and red bows. The table cloth is made from white, old country lace, tatted by an elder long passed.

When the meal is ready, each matriarch begins placing their masterpieces on the dinner table. The feast will begin with baccala pasta salad, the salted cod and spaghetti noodles providing the perfect marriage of starch and fish drowning in homemade Italian dressing with fresh herbs. Any Italian cook worth her heritage uses the fresh herbs that she grows in her window to include basil, oregano and parsley. A truly devout Catholic also raises marjoram, thyme and lavender. It is a rule. Somewhere. The marinated eel and fried smelts will be placed as appetizers around the house. The actual meal, the one they will all sit down for, will be four kinds of pastas with bolognese, alfredo, caprese and red sauce. This gathering of Italians will stuff themselves with dense, heavy, garlic bread and steamed scallops, fried and broiled calamari, stuffed, baked quahogs and the beloved puttanesca which is little more than anchovies in tomato sauce.

Every person in the house will eat and eat like the Grinch at the Who Feast. Wine will be diminished by the gallon with talk of mama and papa, a sign of the Cross and a "God rest their souls".

Gifts are exchanged, another 32-36 cheek kisses and Vinnie and Analisa are heading home, Christmas Eve #39 in the books. But on this night, the Lord's night, Vinnie has one more gift to wrap up.

RX for Revenge

Steven can't believe he has not passed out. His arms
are cramping and he is in unbearable pain. His wrists
are tied together and hoisted over his head. He is
suspended from a meat hook with his feet just inches
from the floor. The doctor has enough training under
his belt to know this is intentional, a head game
sadists like to play,keeping you inches from escape.

The men who brought him here have cut off his shirt
and his Armani dress slacks are now stained with
urine. He has somehow managed not to soil them
with feces. He determines not to give his captors the
satisfaction of that act. Curious the things we take
pride in during the last moments of our existence.

Steven does not recognize the men who jumped him
as he tried to enter his home this evening. Even so,
he knows why they took him and he knows they are
friends of Vinnie's. By some miracle, Vinnie has
escaped mob justice and now he will exact his
revenge on the good doctor. This much, Steven
understands.

The door in the warehouse swings open and in
swaggers Vincent Castana.

"Hey, Doc!! What's up wid youse? I mean besides
youse!" Vinnie laughs heartily at his own joke. Steven
begins to wimper.

"Vince............." But he never finishes the second
syllable because Vinnie stuffs a dirty rag in his mouth.
Steven gags against it and swallows a teaspoon of
vomit.

"Youse see, Doc. Youse messed up. Youse took me for a chump. And I ain't nobody's chump, Doc. I can't let you beg for your miserable life tonight, because I know you will try some more of your funny mind bidness on me and I can't be havin'it."

Vinnie does not seem stupid now. Vinnie is mighty pleased with himself. Steven mumbles through his gag desperate to speak.

"What's that youse say?" Vinnie laughs again.

"I will give youse this, Doc. Youse are very good at youse job. Youse had me fooled. But I am also good at my bidness, Doc. Youse might not know it, but I do my research and I take my assignments seriously. I study. I study the art of death. I have something unique and special planned for youse my friend. Have youse ever heard of the blood eagle, Doc?"

Vinnie's eyes hold an enthusiasm Steven has not seen in him before this moment. He shakes his head no to answer Vinnie.

Then Vinnie walks away leaving the good doctor to ponder the possibilities. He crosses the warehouse floor and approaches Carmine and Nicky, his gorillas.

Nicky speaks first,

"You sitting sideline tonight, Vin?"

"No, Nicky, I am front and center for this one," Vinnie replies.

This one here is the eighth fish of the evening.

Carmine continues,

"Vinnie, what did you have in mind?"

"Boys, wese about to go Viking on this mother #@%*#@!"

Epilogue-Episode One

(PJ and Brad)

Peyton is nursing lukewarm coffee with no girl creamer (*French vanilla*) while she reads the obituary page. She was not as satisfied as she thought she would be when she read that Dr. Fisher was missing and now she is emotionless, scanning his obit. PJ thought she would feel more if this ever happened. God knows that she wished it on him many times. She does feel a bit relieved that Steven would not be able to make good on his threat to tell Brad. It took a while for the memory of her confrontation with him to return. Then she felt bad for thinking of herself first.

Because she is a Christian, she will hold a feeling of guilt about celebrating his death.

Vengeance is mine, sayeth the Lord.

And Peyton believes that down to her middle.

It has been months since she was his patient and even a few days since she had given what he did to her any real time in her mind. PJ is skilled at forgiveness and she is thankful that Brad did not discover her potential indiscretion. She truly loves the man.

So, on she went with her life, content and feeling as though she had dodged a bullet. Peyton lowers the morning paper and walks to the kitchen to start Brad's breakfast. She grabs a package of eggs from the refrigerator and lays them on the granite counter. She rubs the counter slowly, it reminds her of her childhood in Virginia when she would balance herself precariously on creek rocks of rust, yellow and black. That memory is what prompted her to choose this particular pattern and she enjoys this daily stroll back in time. She moves the frying pan on the stovetop to the front burner and turns the heat to medium. Returning to the refrigerator, she grabs unsalted butter and milk.

PJ reaches into the cabinet for a Pfaltzgraf bowl and into the drawer for a rubber-coated whisk. She opens the eggs and carefully cracks three on the side of the bowl delicately dropping the liquid interior the way the chefs on the cooking shows do. PJ opens the milk and adds a brief splash to the eggs, then she grinds fresh pepper and adds a pinch of sea salt. She takes the whisk, balances the bowl under her left arm and starts whipping the mixture.

When the froth begins to form on the top, she sets the bowl down and grabs the butter. She slices off a generous portion and sizzles it into the warming pan. Once it has completely liquified, she will add the eggs.

She turns away from the stove to put on some coffee and when she looks up, she sees her husband. The look of defeat on his face is devastating and she instantly worries about one of the kids or a parent having been in an accident.

"What? Brad? What is it?"

Then she sees it in his hand. Her diary. A geyser of dread wells up inside her rising and rising until it will blow her to bits. Words she cannot speak choke in the water in her throat.

Brad speaks first.

"I didn't mean to read it, Peege. I was looking under the bath cabinet for an extra bar of soap and it fell out and opened on the floor. At first, I thought I was reading a love letter written for me. Wasn't long before I figured it out."

Brad doesn't look angry, just profoundly sad. He continues,

"How long have you been seeing him?"

 PJ starts to answer but Brad does not let her in.

"But before you answer, I am not sure why it matters because five minutes is too long, but it does matter. It so matters, Peege. And I am sure his real name is not Cyrano, so maybe we can start there."

:

Epilogue – Episode Two

(Vinnie)

Dr. Fisher has been missing for three weeks now. Miss Honeycut has done all that she could to maintain his practice hoping that he would return. She is fielding calls, making up excuses and covering for her missing employer in any way possible.

The phone call confirming the DNA result on the torso that was discovered floating in the Hudson River has all but defeated her. His death is not the source of her anxiety, it is the loss of her position with this office. She tells the detective investigating Steven's disappearance that she will clean up around the place and if she discovers anything of importance, she will immediately forward the information to him.

So she has gone about her day, cleaning out old files and her desk and stalling her exit for as long as possible. It is now time to attack Steven's desk. For some reason, she dreads the thought of doing it. She holds no affection for him, she just finds it creepy. He is now a dead man and she is rifling through his things.

She enters the office, switches on the chandelier and crosses to the desk. She opens the file drawer to the right of his chair and flips through the contents. She sees the files of current and former patients, all of whom she has contacted to inform them that their appointments need to be rescheduled or that Dr. Fisher is no longer seeing them. Now she will have to call each one again, at least the current patients, to inform them that the practice has terminated. What will she say? She has no idea.

My chauvinistic, narcissistic slave driver boss pisses off the wrong guy and gets drawn and quartered for it. Even he did not deserve what they did to him.

Miss Honeycut begins to softly sob, not for Steven so much as for herself. She suddenly realizes the magnitude of her task and is determined to continue. She removes the files from the drawer and places them into a cardboard file box where she will sort them later.

She closes the file drawer and slides open the center drawer of the hickory desk. She pushes around some paper clips, a few coins, a lip balm and a small set of keys. Honeycut picks up Steven's expensive writing utensil and writes her name on the calendar lying on top of his desk.

"I'll keep this," she says to herself as she pockets it in the front of her blouse. She places both hands underneath the drawer and starts to push it back in towards the starting point when she feels something strange in her hand. She pulls the drawer back towards her and reaches underneath to release a paper object that is trapped under the drawer. When it does not immediately release, she ducks her head under and sees it is secured with duct tape on both ends. She loosens the grasp of the tape against the letter and removes it from its temporary tomb.

Honeycut turns it over and over in her hands, afraid to open it. The outside statement on the envelope is concise and to the point:

IN THE EVENT OF MY UNTIMELY DEMISE OR IN
THE EVENT I AM MISSING, PLEASE OPEN AND
READ

*How could he have known? Was he aware he was
being stalked? Who did he think was after him?*

Honeycut is at first afraid to open the envelope and
afraid not to open it. Whatever her boss had gotten
himself into, she wants no part of it. But her curious
nature takes hold of her and she cannot resist. She
rips open the envelope and reads:

To Whom It Might Concern at This Juncture,

He always sounds like a lawyer.

I, Dr. Steven Francis Fisher, Licensed Therapist, have
been treating one Vincent Castana since March of
2016 here in my office for an anxiety related health
issue. During the course of his treatment, Mr.
Castana, who has significant ties to the mob and is a
current employee as such, has made several thinly
veiled threats to my safety. As a result, I have
recorded audio tapes of our sessions which revealed
many past transgressions to include maimings and
the actual murder of 17 individuals. I have comprised
this list as a precautionary item in the hope it will keep
me from harm. If you are reading this, then I have
come to some unnatural end, and I would ask you to
forward it to the proper authorities. All of the
transcripts of our sessions as well as the tapes and a
second list of victims and how they were executed
can be located in the wall safe behind the Pollock
painting. The keys to this safe are in the center

drawer where this letter was located. Thank you. Dr. Steven F. Fisher, MD

Attached to the letter, Honeycut found a detailed mob hit list that read like a headline along with the actual method of each one's demise:

1) Carmine Castella: beaten to death with pipes
2) Nicky Fiorina: drowned off the Jersey shore with his feet in cement
3) Frankie Malone: bullet to the back of the head
4) Iceman Kuklinski: drawn and quartered
5) Joey Barbato: strangled with wire
6) James Di Giovanni: castrated and beaten to death
7) Leoni Moceri: stabbed multiple times
8) Frank Diamond: sawn in half
9) Nucky Jackson: burned alive
10) Alphonse Giaccone: bullet to the back of the head
11) Simon Onofrio: bullet to the back of the head
12) Stanley Koury: dropped in a vat of acid
13) Scotty Squitieri: drowned in a hot tub
14) Brian Battaglia: head crushed in a vice
15) Dominic Hoff: drive by shooting
16) Leonardo Todaro: tied naked to a tree
17) Tommy O' Toole: beaten and decapitated with a stiletto

Honeycut sits back in the leather chair and sighs, processing all that has been laid at her feet. She opens the drawer for a final time, retrieves the set of keys and walks to the Pollock. Honeycut is not aware of any wall safe before this moment. She pulls at the left side of the painting. Nothing. She pulls at the right side of the painting. Nothing. She grabs it with both hands and tries to pull it toward her. Nothing. She turns and leans against it, rethinking her strategy for opening it. She interlaces her fingers and pushes her arms out, her day has been long and her muscles are exhausted. As she stretches them out, she feels the painting give way just a bit vertically. She turns back to the Pollock, places both hands gingerly at the bottom of the frame and gently glides it upward revealing a small metal safe. She inserts the key and turns the lock until it clicks. The door pops open on its own. Inside she locates the files, the tapes, the transcripts and the second copy of the hit list. Each name is listed and beside the listing the manner in which Vinnie chose to dispose of them-all from Vinnie's own mouth while under hypnosis. Honeycut also discovers the missing mob money.

Honeycut leaves Steven's office and grabs another cardboard file box. She places all the "evidence" inside, tapes it up tight, and addresses the box to the detective. She ponies the box down to the mail room with the instruction to "rush" it. Honeycut returns to the vault, removes a small tin box, extracts several bundles of hundreds and places them in her purse. She closes the vault, tosses the keys in her pocket, lowers the Pollock and switches off the chandelier. She strolls out of the office of Dr. Steven Fisher for the final time.

Epilogue – Episode Three

(Calliope)

Jeff is sleeping. Baby boy Seaton has kept him up most of the night and so Calliope tip-toes around her husband so he can catch up on his rest. Little Man will be three weeks old tomorrow and he is starting to get his little personality. Calliope had no idea how much she could love 8 pounds of child. She feels the same way every new parent feels, all those trite statements people make about the miracle of birth. Her son is perfect. Just like everyone else's.

Her delivery was routine. Mt. Sinai did the honors. Her labor was intensely painful but without any risk and her child entered his new world healthy and strong.

They call him Rocky which is the closest Jeff would let her get to Rocket. She is grateful that Jeff is a big Stallone fan or Rocky would have been off the table. And it fits him. He is a chunky little nugget. His arms are so generous it looks like someone put rubber bands around his wrists.

He has Jeff's hair and cleft chin but the nose she can claim. Rocky has a head full of dark hair and his eyes are crystal blue. Jeff tells her that his dad shares the same color. Jeff loves seeing his parents manifest themselves on his son.

Rocky coos from his rocket bed and his mother hurries to his side. He smiles up at his beautiful mother eating his own face away. Cee Cee lifts her son from his bed and lays him on her right shoulder, patting his back. Rocky holds his head up for the first time by himself. He blinks against the morning just long enough to display a perfectly formed duodent interrupting the blue.

Made in the USA
Lexington, KY
06 April 2017